IORA & THE QUEST of FIVE

Playing with snakes, exploring unknown caves and treading jungles has always delighted Arefa as much as penning down words. Honorary Wildlife Warden of Udaipur and a non-conformist, Arefa is a reading, travel and wildlife enthusiast. She hails from a multicultural and multi-religious family and has contributed column, features, research notes, stories, poems and articles to national and international publications. She is the co-author of *Tales from the Wild* and has other titles scheduled to be published including fiction, non-fiction and wildlife edutainment books.

Published by
FiNGERPRINT!
An imprint of Prakash Books India Pvt. Ltd.

113/A, Darya Ganj,
New Delhi-110 002
Tel: (011) 2324 7062 – 65, Fax: (011) 2324 6975
Email: info@prakashbooks.com/sales@prakashbooks.com

facebook www.facebook.com/fingerprintpublishing
twitter www.twitter.com/FingerprintP
www.fingerprintpublishing.com

Edited by Sonalini Chaudhry

ISBN: 978 81 7234 416 0

Printed and bound in India by Nutech Photolithographers

IORA & THE QUEST of FIVE

AREFA TEHSIN

FiNGERPRINT!

Dedication

To my dad, Dr Raza H Tehsin, who gave me in abundance the greatest gift a child can get – time.

Acknowledgement

Thank you . . .

Adityavikram More, for making me realise my love for writing.

Himalay Tehsin, for being my first editor and critic.

Sonalini Chaudhry, for believing in Iora.

Contents

1
Girl in the Rainforest

"Look at that girl in the jungle, Papa!" exclaimed Chinar, standing on the deck of the boat. "Hurry!" he shouted at the top of his voice, bending low on the railing.

"What is it, Chinar? And don't you lean so low!" roared Dr Reddy, much to the surprise of his research assistant, Hamza, who followed him from the cabin.

"Stop the boat! There is a little girl behind those trees!"

"Are you sure, Son?" asked Dr Reddy. "I've not heard of any kind of jungle people staying in these parts." His husky voice rang with authority.

But Chinar was too caught up with the excitement. "Oh yes, I'm sure! She hid behind that tree."

"Okay. Even if there is one, why do you want to stop the boat?" frowned Dr Reddy.

"Sir, we c-can perhaps go check on the river b-bank . . ."

stammered Hamza, looking nervous in the professor's company.

"Yes, Sir, let's check this out. Perhaps someone needs rescuing," joined another assistant, who had come out holding a plant and a bottle of preservative.

"Alright, alright! We'll do a quick check. Ask the captain to steer the boat to where Chinar has supposedly seen someone."

Adjusting his thick spectacles, Dr Reddy took Chinar aside as the boat was steered towards the bank.

"Look, Chinar," he said in an undertone, "since you were just four years old, I have brought you along on expeditions to start your training early. This is not a picnic! Your mother has not come this time. But that does not mean you're allowed to run amok!"

"But, Papa, I did see this girl. She has long, black, curly hair . . ."

"Enough!" said Dr Reddy. "Our job is to explore the rainforest for new plant species. Even if we see jungle dwellers, we are not interested in them! Have I made myself very clear?"

Chinar nodded, scuffing the toes of his shoe on the deck rails.

The giant, ruddy rainforest river curved leisurely like a giant boa slithering along the forest; the water rippled and sparkled in the sun like the boa's scales. Clouds began to gather overhead, masking the afternoon sun as Hamza, Chinar and some of the crew stepped ashore before the row of massive trees standing guard to the forest beyond. They looked high and low and ventured as deep as they safely could, but not a soul was in sight.

Tap-tap-tap, big droplets of water hit the leaves.

"Have we wasted enough time already?" Dr Reddy hollered from the long, well-equipped boat.

"Come back, Chinar!" cried Hamza, as he headed back to the boat with the others.

"Just a minute . . . let me look behind that tree . . ." said Chinar, running towards the row of trees.

Suddenly, the rain began to fall down in dense sheets of water. It was as if someone had upturned a gigantic bucket in the sky. The row of trees swayed with the wind like bad-tempered ghosts nailed to the ground. It seemed they were trying to break free from the shackles of thick, wide-leafed vines gripping their trunks and branches.

"Chinar, come back at once!" Dr Reddy yelled.

Ka-boooooom! Lightning flashed, accompanying the rumbling thunder, as it tore the sky.

"Help . . ." Chinar's cry was drowned in the howling gale.

"Chinar . . ." another cry came from the river, gushing past the rainforest. It shoved and pushed the white and blue boat in its ruddy waters.

"Stop the boat! Chinar is still on the shore!" cried Dr Reddy.

"Professor . . . the captain c-can't control the b-boat . . ."

said Hamza, looking terrified and balancing himself as the boat hurtled further down the river.

Thunder roared and lightning made erratic webs overhead. A wall of water rose and banged into the boat, making those in it slip from one end to the other.

"Sir . . . I think that is Chinar running on the shore!" said the other research assistant looking hard through the heavy rain.

"I can't see clearly . . . my glasses . . . all this rain . . ."

Dr Reddy strained his eyes and saw a small figure running near the bank in the rainforest. "Chinar!" he cried at the top of his voice.

Krrrr . . . Bang! A terrifying sound, like a trumpeting elephant, resounded through the raging storm. An old fig tree, big enough to provide wood for Noah's Ark, crashed in the river just in front of the little figure. Half of it fell in the river, sending towering waves up into the air.

"No . . . this can't b-be ha-happening!" Hamza exclaimed, as the cruiser was washed away into the high currents.

Dr Reddy stood speechless, his hands clutching bloodlessly at the rails . . .

****

After a couple of hours, the bright blue sky was calm like a meditating hermit. Only some fallen trees on the ground betrayed the destruction it had caused moments back. A tall, well-built man wearing greenish-brown shorts and leather straps on his chest helped a chubby girl with thick, curly, black hair out of a cave.

Inside the forest, the light was an odd faint green, the sky blotted out due to the dense foliage overhead. Thick loops of lianas hung from the trees, their cords binding the jungle.

The clothes of the man and the girl turned mud-coloured. The man, carrying a twig in his hand, broke the silence.

"No need to feel bad, dear. Everything will be just fine. As a child, even I had once attracted the attention of non-jungle dwellers. Chameleon skin clothes saved me then too," he said, looking gratefully down at his shorts. Their clothes changed colour according to the background as they walked. "Never forget to put them on when you leave Twitterland."

The girl didn't answer him.

"Wait," he said, and climbed up a tree, which had diverse aerial plants growing on the branches and trunk, to pluck some berries. There were cisterns on the trunk, filled with clear water. The man climbed down comfortably, holding the lianas.

"Here, now smile . . ." he said, handing over the berries to her.

"Sorry, Father," said the girl, "I could have moved out quickly if I had not stopped to stare at the strange float."

"Don't worry. We managed to run away before they got down from the float. I hope they left before the storm."

"But why don't we make friends with them like all

the other forest creatures?"

"Because they are not forest creatures."

"But we look quite similar."

"We are different. My little blabbermouth, you can't stop asking questions, can you?"

"I saw some purple-faced monkeys on the river bank. Their talkative lot will tell them all about us!"

"Don't you worry, non-jungle dwellers can't speak to animals."

"Can't what?"

"Yes, my orchid. For them, we are just a lost civilisation . . ."

Right in the middle of the jungle they stopped in front of an unusually thick foliage. In a dark corner there were some large crystal orchid leaves, resembling a bowl, into which water fell from a crystal orchid suspended on a slimy rock.

2
Twitterland

"Let me do it, Father . . ." said the little girl rolling her eyes.

"Okay, honeybee." He lifted her up to the rock on which the crystal orchid was suspended. The little girl reached up, bent the rock as if it were a rubber stick, and placed the crystal orchid in the crystal bowl. There was a faint humming sound. Slowly, the four-five hundred feet tall trees swayed in their places. The thick vines began to part and go back into the ground, bringing the sunlight in. The dampness of the rainforest evaporated.

Two wing-shaped branches that had blocked the vision before, opened up gently, and revealed a stone pathway leading to a town square. A crystal paradise bird was placed in the middle of a pond. Sunrays fell on it emitting rainbow colours, which reflected on the surrounding stone cottages. The crystal bird stood on one leg, its feathers spread and beak pointing upwards, about to take off in flight.

As far as eyes could see, there was a wall of tall trees surrounding Twitterland. A couple of Okapis, marble white horse-like creatures with black stripes on their thighs and rear, trotted around. The red crystal roofs of the stone cottages were bowl shaped to store rainwater. This water would later be used for chores around the house – cleaning, cooking and more.

A single cloud hung low above Twitterland, drifting slowly and making different forms. This was the Mystic Mist. Inside the town were many trees, some laden with flowers, others with fruits. At a distance, there was an emerald-coloured lake where all the streams pooled together. The placid waters of the lake reflected the green blanket of plants and trees that circled its shores.

"Where have you been, Heron? On another outing with little Iora?" asked a bearded, bony man sitting at the town square.

"That's right, Kookaburra."

"Don't you think it is a bit early to teach her things in the jungle? Don't Gurukuls hold any importance for you at all?"

"I hold them in very high regard. This is just a little prelude," Heron answered, smiling.

"Oh, we had such a thrilling experience when I spotted . . ." started Iora.

"Little one, you can narrate that later. Grandpa must be waiting," said Heron.

Heron and Iora bid farewell to Kookaburra and went towards a cottage situated just near the lake.

"Another training adventure, huh?" chirped a red, flame-backed woodpecker, sitting on the roof of their house. A spotless white okapi grazed on leaves in the front garden. He curtsied with a gentle dip and Heron patted him on the back.

"You wouldn't believe . . ." started Iora, but the woodpecker cut in and said, "Yes I wouldn't believe you, alright. What do you expect when your father takes such an extraordinary girl to train her in all crazy things? I was such a talented bird but my parents didn't take me out flying when I was two days old! Oh . . . I've become the family bird of the wrong, wrong family . . ."

"I am not two days old . . . I am eleven years old!" Iora retorted to the ranting woodpecker.

"Oh come now, Madame Flameback," interrupted Heron. "You can have a nice hot coffee. If it was not for you, Iora wouldn't be called Little Incredible Twitter, would she?"

"No coffee drink, but yes, some coffee beans would be fine," said Madame Flameback, following them inside their cottage, with a flick of her wings.

A short tree stood in the middle of the kitchen. Its branches spread throughout the house, running close under the ceiling. A fat wooden face smiled from its trunk.

"Hope you got some coffee beans from the forest. Old Cockatoo is fuming!" it said, moving some of its branches to arrange the table.

"Thank you, Bungee Banyan," said Heron, taking out the coffee beans.

Sitting on a wooden armchair, in the hall overlooking the emerald lake, was an old man. He wore a fluffy bathrobe and an unyielding expression.

"I was wondering how long you are going to make an old man wait for his coffee . . ."

A crooked walking stick was placed on one side of the chair. With a bent back, and unnaturally thick, brown, curly hair for an old man, Cockatoo was not exactly the most favourite company in Twitterland. Not that he was nasty but he was so stern that he seemed to be looking down on everyone else. The only people he relented to were his son Heron, his granddaughter Iora and his friend Kookaburra.

Before Heron could stop Iora, she blurted, "I saw non-jungle dwellers!"

"What!" shrieked Madame Flameback and stared at the old man as he stared back at her. The happy expression on Bungee Banyan's face vanished and all its leaves stood pointed toward the ceiling, stretched and so erect that it seemed they would break any minute.

"Now what have you been up to?" asked the old man with a raised eyebrow.

"We saw them accidentally, Father," answered Heron.

"Did *they* accidentally see you?"

"Well, only Iora. A little boy did see her, but for a very short while, only a little flash really. I am sure they were convinced it was just an illusion."

"They better be!" said Madame Flameback, clicking her claws on the table.

"They can never find us. They haven't known of our existence for thousands of years and even today the rainforests are quite impenetrable for them," replied a defensive Heron.

The angry cloud that hung over the elders was thicker than the Mystic Mist, thought Iora; she slipped quietly into her room to change.

"They kill what we worship and destroy the jungles we live in!" said the old man, seething.

"With all due respect, Father, I don't think they can destroy the jungles completely. The Angels of Nature will not let it happen."

"So, young man, next you'll be making friends with them! Wrong, wrong family I've been put into!" said Madame Flameback, as Heron gave her some fragrant coffee beans.

Iora sneaked out of the house and went to the fruit garden just behind the shrine. There were different vine swings and the trees and shrubs were laden with strawberries, dragon fruits, raspberries, kiwis, jackfruits and jujubes. Two Tatzelwurms did the gardening. They were long, five to six feet thick worms with round faces and two stubby hands.

"Can I have an orange, please?" asked Iora, as she reached out to pluck one from a tree.

"Yes, but throw the seeds in the garden," said the tree, opening its woody eyes and lowering one of its branches, "I need more saplings. These watermelons are utterly dominating the garden space!"

After she had strewn some orange seeds on a patch of soil, Iora walked towards a group of children playing near the pond.

"What did you do on your outing today?" asked a girl.

"You'll know soon enough. Remember . . . today is the moonless night," said Iora.

"Ooooh! Someone is being all hush-hush," said a straight-haired boy, trying to get the hair out of his eyes.

"You want us to disobey your father, Owlus? He has told us to keep our learning to ourselves till the gathering. We try to ape each other otherwise."

"Who will try to ape *you,* Iora? What do you have except an eccentric grandpa and a jungle wanderer father?" sniggered a boy with buck-teeth.

Most of them seemed weary of his talk but his brother giggled, exposing the gap where his two front teeth should've been. Owlus sneered.

"Well, at least we have our teeth in place," Iora said, eating the rest of the orange.

"Shh . . . Iora . . ." came a thin voice from behind a shrub. All the children fell silent and looked in that direction. A short, stout, dark-skinned man with a bulging stomach, very long hair and beard stood with a bag of twines hanging from his shoulder. He wore his long beard wrapped around his waist instead of clothing. A girl let out a shriek as he smiled at them exposing a set of sharp, neatly laid teeth.

3
Beetle Agogwe

"It's an Agogwe!" muttered a plump boy.

"Yes, he's not supposed to meet the children alone!"

"Hey, don't be scared you all! This is my friend, Beetle Agogwe," said Iora, as she went and stood by his side. Their heights were almost the same; rather the Agogwe looked a little shorter.

"Wait till I tell Father, Iora making friends with Agogwes, huh! We're just allowed to barter jungle products with them," whispered Owlus.

"And only the elders can do that! We kids have no business with them. These are insect worshippers. Next we'll know she has made friends with the Ghosts of Yellow Leaves!" joined the boy with buck teeth.

All the other children gasped at the mention of the Ghosts of Yellow Leaves.

"I thought she was only kidding when she once

mentioned this . . . thing," said a girl.

"How are you, Beetle? I could never imagine you'd meet me in front of other people," said Iora, as they walked away from the gaping group.

"I went to your backyard and tapped at your window but didn't find you. The nasty storm today . . . I knew Heron would be taking you out. Thought I'd check on you," he said, looking kindly at her.

"You know what, I saw . . . umm . . . I saw non-jungle dwellers!"

"Wha . . .?"

"Yes! Yes! I did!"

"Heron . . ."

"Father was with me. There was this kid. They looked so much like us!"

"They are different. They can't communicate with trees or animals."

"But nor can we. I still can't speak to so many of them. See, Father is teaching me snake calls these days."

"Yes, we can't speak to all forest dwellers, but Jungly is our common language and is understood by many. It's great if you know a creature's specific calls, and for someone as proficient as you are in picking up languages, it will be easy-breezy!" said Beetle. "But non-jungle dwellers don't understand Jungly. They are very different from you and me, Iora."

"Hmmm . . ."

"Ah! I remember an Amazon saying she had spotted

some a few days back; wonder if they were the same group," he added.

"Wow . . . did you meet an Amazon? Aren't you afraid of them?"

"Well . . . those lady warriors do not exactly soothe the nerves of a little guy like me, but then one should know how to deal with them."

"And how does one deal with them?" asked Iora, walking by Beetle's side.

They had reached the other end of the lake, where there was a vegetable garden. Some Tatzelwurms fertilised, trimmed and watered the garden. Beyond the vegetable garden was the tree wall, where this side of Twitterland ended. Eagles were posted at different tree levels to guard the vegetables from raiding animals.

One of the eagles spotted Beetle and shouted, "Hey, Agogwe! How is your Insect Angel doing? Tell him I will make a meal of him someday!" Other eagles laughed out aloud.

"Ignore him," said Iora. "He does not spare even us! Owlus's family bird after all!"

"Who let this clumsy Agogwe in?" snapped a tomato creeper, curling its leaves from below Beetle's feet.

"I'm so sorry," said Beetle, getting up on the stone path by the side. He turned to Iora. "You must run along now, dear. I'll leave."

"But you still have to tell me how to deal with the Amazons," persisted Iora.

"Now, now! Run along home, the coffee time rain is going to start," said Beetle.

He turned towards the tree wall and started to climb.

"See you soon. Hope you bring your wife and little one next time," shouted Iora, and ran away from there, wondering how little would his little one be.

Iora crossed the garden on her way home. All the children had left by then.

Grandpa Cockatoo sat in the front porch puffing on a long bamboo pipe. "Beetle Agogwe had come looking for you. Owlus was announcing it to all of Twitterland. I have my reputation to care for but you and your father just don't see it!" he said, fixing his annoyed gaze on Iora as she came along.

None of her famous tantrums would work with him, so she sat in the garden and quietly sulked.

Iora frowned as she saw Kookaburra walking in his shuffling gait towards the porch. Kookaburra was the only friend her Grandpa Cockatoo had in Twitterland. She had often thought that they suited each other quite well.

"Iora, you keep surprising everyone in Twitterland with your odd set of friends," he said, entering the garden.

"There's nothing odd with Beetle!" snapped Iora, and went inside the house.

Cockatoo shook his head and took a long puff.

"Such an unusual child," said Kookaburra.

"It's Heron's training. He may not realise it, but it is grooming her to fear nothing."

"No, Cockatoo, I don't think it's just Heron. They say I'm a sceptic, but I say I observe things more deeply. Do you remember the night she was born? There was a full moon and it was emitting a bluish light. The jungle was very still as if awaiting some news."

Cockatoo looked at him incredulously.

"Don't look at me like that, Cockatoo! You people don't remember because you don't observe. When this girl does all sorts of strange things, I can't help but think – does this augur good or bad?"

"Oh, come on now! Would you like to have a chocolate drink or morning dew? Bungee Banyan has made some good chocolate today."

"Ah! No . . . no chocolate; some morning dew sounds just right," Kookaburra said entering the house. "We have to reach the hall for the festivities before the first planet comes out."

4
The Moonless Night Festivities

Twitters had gathered along with their family birds in the beak-shaped hall. As a custom, all the children under twelve years of age presented what they'd learnt from their parents in the past month. And then would follow a sumptuous dinner. Twitterland didn't have children above the age of twelve. They had been sent to Gurukuls for training in jungle life.

The entire Twitterland was lit up with firefly lamps, which floated in the air. The crystal bird in the town square was surrounded by these firefly lamps too, and they flew up and down. This made the crystal bird's reflection flap wings against the dark sky.

Kookaburra sat in a corner observing everything suspiciously. The children had gathered near the stage to present their learning one by one. A straight-haired girl, who looked remarkably like Owlus, stood near him, rehearsing her presentation.

"Fowlus, for Angel's sake! Stop buzzing like a trapped bee!" snapped Owlus.

"You forget I am older than you, Owlus!"

"Barely one year! Hope you're not sent to Gurukul with me!"

The handsome Heron sat with his father Cockatoo. Damsels eyed him hopelessly as he greeted everyone, but minded his own business.

One of the girls whispered, "Oh my Feathery Angel! Just look at how Heron holds himself. You would think he's the Chieftain!"

"Come now, we all know he was unanimously elected the Chieftain and he denied the post."

"She's right," joined another. "If his wife had not died mysteriously leaving him an infant to take care of, he would have been the Chieftain today. I admire his courage."

Owlus and Fowlus rehearsed their presentation and Owlus scowled at Iora, who helped others practise. His family eagle sat with his head held high and stiff back looking superior and downright mean. A large owl, with two pointed ears, walked around grumpily to make the children stand in a line. Toucan, a strong-built Twitter with zig-zagged teeth, sat with his two sons. The one with buck teeth was Hornbill and the one with missing teeth was Thornbill – the best buddies of Owlus.

The Chieftain Fisherking, Owlus's father, finally

approached the stage and welcomed everyone. People were seated around circular stone tables. After his address, the grumpy owl invited the youngest children one by one. Reciting calls of various birds and insects was what they mostly did.

Now it was the turn of children belonging to Iora's age group to perform. The elders applauded all the performances, even if the children faltered. Some three-toed sloths, slow moving, grey-coloured mammals with their perpetually smiling faces, lean bodies and long nails, entered the hall holding wooden trays. They started serving the Nightqueen flower juice.

"Great! Today the sloths have been called for catering . . . Don't count on getting your dinner before dawn!" grumbled Cockatoo, picking up a fizzy cube.

Owlus came on the stage and the hall was hushed. He had learnt some difficult things this month and itched to perform. He was confident he would outshine Iora today. A sloth came unhurriedly and placed a large box on a table in front of Owlus.

"I am going to demonstrate how to train army ants to rid our surroundings of pests. After that I will . . ." He paused hearing a boy shriek.

He looked down at the box, the lid of which he had just opened. Instead of army ants, the sloth had mistakenly placed a box containing an oddly swollen and venomous snake! The serpent came out, hissing with a vengeance.

The children standing near the stage panicked, all family birds flew overhead, the elders hurried to take the children away, and the utterly slow sloths displayed unusual speed in getting out. The snake slithered towards a group of children. Fisherking, who was a little further off, recovered in a moment after the initial surprise and quickly tried to talk to the snake in Jungly. But clearly it didn't understand the language, or didn't want to understand.

"Move away, Owlus!" Fisherking shouted from his table. But Owlus was frozen in his place. Heron quickly came forward but halted looking at Toucan, who was just near the stage, rushing towards the hissing snake with a pointed branch torn from a Magnolia tree. He attacked the snake and punctured it again and again.

"Stop it, Toucan!" shouted Heron. "We can just capture it!"

Heron didn't like the loathing everyone felt towards snakes and he tried his best not to kill them. But it was too late. The snake had been stabbed and punctured at many places. It lay limp on the floor. Toucan held it up triumphantly for everyone to see, wiping sweat from his forehead in one dramatic sweep. Owlus stood on the stage transfixed. Toucan flung the dead snake into the box and came down from the stage, smiling triumphantly.

Slow murmurs broke through the silence. Twitters started to settle in their seats, exclaiming at what had happened. Just then, a loud, clattering noise grabbed their attention. It seemed that the dead snake had come to life and was lashing out fanatically in the box. From the punctured holes in the snake's body, they saw a shower of baby snakes fly out in all directions as it went around in circles. It was swollen because it was pregnant! That was why it had attacked when disturbed. Everyone stood rooted to their positions, horrified as the baby snakes slithered in all directions. After ejecting at least eighteen baby snakes, the furiously shaking box came to a still. The snake inside had now died, making sure its offspring survived.

5
Worm in the Well

It was a worse situation than before. The baby snakes were poisonous and it was very difficult to corner and kill these fast-moving creatures. They were tiny and could easily disappear in crevices all around; they were slippery and fast and carried a deadly poison. Toucan stood there, lost for words, with the branch raised in his shaking hand.

"Run!" someone shouted.

The whole gathering panicked, much more than before. Some of the Twitters turning on their heels halted hearing a hissing sound amidst them. Iora had started to move towards the stage hissing at a rising pitch. All the slithering snake babies stopped, so did the Twitters rushing out. Iora went to the stage, removed the dead snake from the box and placed it a little away, while hissing constantly. The baby snakes began to come towards her and then went inside the box one by one. Heron also came on the stage and stood next to the box. He hissed in a low tone with her. As soon as the last baby snake went inside the box, Heron closed the lid.

For a few moments everyone stood transfixed but as soon as the Fisherking exclaimed "Bravo!", the whole gathering broke into a relieved applause. Owlus stood frowning. Only Iora's presentation remained after his, and her presence of mind and making the snake calls was more than impressive. Many Twitters patted her on her head. Heron joined his father who sat at his place, unmoved by all the drama that had everybody alert on their toes.

The evening progressed with sloths serving dinner out in the open, around a large bonfire. Deer-milk pudding, quail eggs in lily sauce, barbequed crabs and flavoured raindrops were the night's specialities.

The Mystic Mist had taken the form of a worm. It had misty spikes on its body and moved slowly, curving and straightening like a worm.

"The Bird Angel's blessing is forming a snake," said Madame Flameback.

"And those spikes must be where it was stabbed!" said Fowlus.

"It is not supposed to show things that have already happened, but forewarn about things that are to happen. It is sad that we don't heed the warnings of this premonition cloud placed over Twitterland by the Bird Angel," sighed Kookaburra.

***

The next morning, Iora woke up to find Heron packing his outdoor sack. "Are we going on another outing, Father?"

"No, honeydew. I'm off to a hunting and gathering trip. You can learn about lake vegetation from Grandpa and high-growing fruits from Madame Flameback until I come back."

"But I was really looking forward to another outing . . ."

"I'll be back in no time."

Cockatoo gave Heron a list of things he wanted from the forest. "Better to get it fresh than to barter the stale stuff from the trader. And yes, do try to bring jaguar skin," he said.

"I'm sorry, Father. Can't do that. The jaguars and I have an understanding. If we ever come face to face, we keep to our respective paths."

"I wanted it for my aching knees. They're getting worse! Even Kookaburra's knee is not getting any better . . ." he said, disapproving of Heron's refusal.

"Oh! The teeth of the Black River Piranhas are the best remedy for knee pain. Will try to get those for you," replied Heron.

"But, Father, they're so dangerous . . . much more than normal piranhas! Who can survive after encountering them?" cried Iora.

"Don't you worry, dear, I'll be fine. We can't see Grandpa confined to his armchair, can we?"

"I'll speak to the healer again and ask if he's developed something new," said Cockatoo wearily.

"Oh no, Father, you've spoken to him so many times. There is no other cure for this. I'll leave now, have to cross the Scar-faced River before sundown," said Heron, picking up his bag.

"At least tell me what your plans are," implored Iora.

"Well, I plan to spend a couple of days in the forest on the other side of the Scar-faced River, cross again to this side and then go to the Wacky Wilderness."

Once he'd told Iora about his tentative plan, Heron bade them farewell.

The Mystic Mist still retained its spiky worm look. Iora's day was spent playing with the other children. She led her group of mischief-makers and pulled a prank on Kookaburra, who ran after them, stick in hand, threatening to give them all a sound walloping. And then there was the prank they played on the fat healer. Iora and the others replaced his dry eucalyptus sticks with animal bones. The poor man didn't even realise it was a prank. He laughed aloud at himself for using dry bones on his resentful patient, who was definitely not amused.

Madame Flameback's children had come to visit her from the interior jungle and she was busy stuffing them with honeydew and cocoa-filled dates. Didn't look like Iora would learn anything from her for a few days. She eagerly awaited Hoatzin, the eldest resident of Twitterland. Hoatzin looked ancient but, in fact, her senses had improved with age. Everyone turned to her for advice, even the Chieftain. Rumours had it that she was aware of many secrets of the forest – dark or otherwise. She had been out on a jungle trip for more than a month and was expected back anytime. She always returned with hardly any collections. No one knew what she did for such long intervals in the forest. There was not even a House-Tree to manage the house in her absence. It seemed she was more adapted to jungle life than life in civilisation. If Iora loved learning, it was because of Heron and Hoatzin who taught her exciting things. The other children were a little scared of the strange, old lady.

After dinner, Iora told Grandpa Cockatoo that she had to go to the Blossom Garden as the young Star-flower bush was to flower. “It has promised to present me its first flower!”

The first flower of this bush was special. It acted like a magnifying glass and a telescope all at once. One could look through the flower and observe the sky through this telescope. But sadly, only till the flower withered away.

“Don’t be too late coming back home,” said Cockatoo, as he retreated to his room.

Iora strolled towards the garden and there she saw the fluorescent Mystic Mist taking the shape of a halo. She reached the other end of the town square where there was a flower garden. There were no pollinating bees at this hour. Most of the flowers slept soundly on their branches. Some plants that had cauliflory – flowers growing directly on the stem – slept on their stems. Night flowers emitted soothing fragrances.

"I'm sorry, Iora. I won't be able to flower tonight," rustled the Star-flower bush, as it saw her coming. "Some kid plucked my buds."

"Oh no! Who was this rogue fellow?" Seeing the bush clueless, Iora said, "Hmmm . . . I know you're young and don't know us all as yet. I'll come again tomorrow."

While going back, she passed the lonely cottage of Kookaburra and saw him dozing off on his porch. She was not at all sleepy so she decided to stroll in the backyard of her house.

There was a small well at the end of their back garden, which was near the lake. A curious sound, like a child's giggle, came from somewhere inside it. Iora went in that direction. A vine fully covered the walls of the well. The source of sound was not on the outer wall, so she looked for it in the inner wall.

"Who is it?" she asked but got no reply.

It must be some unknown insect, she thought. She bent down the well, searching the vine with both hands. The insect still made that sound which echoed in the well, confirming that it was somewhere in there.

"Hello, little one, don't hide, no harm intended," she said, bending further down so that only her toes touched the ground.

The vine was fast asleep. There was a gush of wind and Iora lost ground. She tumbled down the well, her voice lost in the howl of the air current. A little branch of the vine came forward and pricked her intentionally as she passed it. She looked back and heard a soft "He! He! He!" It was a tiny worm with thorny appendages that had pricked her. "Rogue Thorn Worm . . ." she uttered softly, splashing on the water. Numbness began spreading in her body and though she was a very good swimmer, she couldn't move her hands or legs. All she could do was hold her breath underwater when she heard a sound above the well. She tried hard to come to the surface and cry for help but felt powerless.

"Dangerous to meet here," came a voice, muffled through the water, strangely familiar.

"Need Heron's blood to proceed," came another piercing voice, quite unpleasant even through the water which softened it.

"Must be done on the next moonless night," said the first voice.

After a chuckle, the sounds stopped. Iora's eyes had popped trying to hold her breath and look through the water. All she saw was a dark shadow retreating. Her eyelids were heavy but she couldn't close them or hold her breath any longer when she felt something rising in front of her. There was a dim light inside due to a few fluorescent stones on the wall. She saw an outline of a water creature with bat-wing like fins that gave it a square shape, and a long, thin but fleshy tail. It closed its fins around Iora and she ached to scream. But her mouth couldn't move even in a silent cry; her eyes and whole body frozen in motionless terror . . .

6 Hoatzin

The creature, with Iora in its embrace, leaped out of the well and dropped her on the grass. On its way down, it pulled the vine along. The vine woke up due to the agonising pull and raised alarm seeing Iora lying stiff near her. Iora heard that sound and lost consciousness.

The next morning, she woke up with the plump healer, Cockatoo and Madame Flameback on her bedside.

"How are you feeling?" asked Cockatoo.

"I feel as if I was frozen and then melted. I don't know if you could feel that way," she said feebly.

"You are just fine, little lady," said the healer.

"Thank you, Feathery Angels!" exclaimed Madame Flameback in relief.

Grandpa Cockatoo fed Iora some dark-green medicine.

"I'll leave now, Cockatoo. Iora, you'll be able to play by tomorrow. But don't you go pulling this stunt for the next moonless night performance! Ha! Ha! Ha!" said the jovial healer, leaving the room.

Iora looked at Grandpa Cockatoo, still not completely in her senses.

"You were bitten by a Rogue Thorn Worm. Knowing the curiosity bug in you, I bet you must have gone after its strange voice first."

"Yes, I think so, Grandpa. Can't remember."

"You were given the antidote just on time. Otherwise, I would have to run around in the jungle looking for your father," he said, as Iora again drifted into sleep.

By the next day, Iora was fit. Now she remembered the happenings of the previous night. She went straight to Grandpa and narrated the incident.

Grandpa Cockatoo listened intently and said, "Now look, you may recall such things since you were bitten by a Rogue Thorn Worm. You may have imagined the voices or you may have amplified any sound in the half-wakeful state. And the creature that removed you from the well could just be a large fish."

"But how could any large fish come in the well?"

"Water is connected through various underground channels. Could have been a stray fish from our adjoining lake," he said, restless to end the discussion.

"Wait . . . that vine, it must have seen the creature! Let's find out."

Grandpa Cockatoo followed her out, frowning as she ran towards the well.

"No . . . I didn't see anyone. I just heard a splash when I woke up. Something seemed to have pulled at me though; must've been a fish," said the vine.

Grandpa Cockatoo looked at Iora and said, "Go play now. My knees are a bit sore. I'll rest for a while before Kookaburra drops by around the coffee time rain."

Iora couldn't believe it was a dream. It seemed too real to her. She went to the healer and asked if there was a possibility of seeing things that didn't happen when she was bitten. He laughed and said it was possible. She spent the whole day going over and over her dream. The words, "Need Heron's blood to proceed", kept ringing in her head. The Mystic Mist formed a cascading waterfall today. She wondered if what it had formed on the moonless night was not a snake but a Rogue Thorn Worm and the halo shape was a prophecy involving the well. She didn't play at all and went to bed early. While retreating to her room, she heard Madame Flameback say to Grandpa Cockatoo, "It'll take her a day or two to recover and then she'll be fine."

The next day, she woke up with the same thoughts. If only her father were here, she thought for the umpteenth time, really missing his wise self.

While she had the breakfast prepared by Bungee Banyan, Madame Flameback flew in chirping, "Cheer up, Iora, your friend Hoatzin returned last night!"

Iora left her unfinished breakfast and ignoring her grandpa's calls, she rushed to Hoatzin's cottage.

In the front garden of the cottage, an old lady, slightly bent, with thick, curly, white hair braided into plaits, trimmed large leaves of a shrub that spread its branches one by one.

"Little Iora has got a lot on her mind today," Hoatzin said, smiling warmly.

She lay down her tools and invited Iora in. Her cottage was unkempt and had various sorts of attacking weeds, hazardous cactuses, wood and stone weaponry, viper and cobra fangs and other deadly objects scattered around the hall. The new addition and the only endearing thing was a baby chimp. She brought some or the other creature from her jungle excursions and returned it to its home again on her next trip. This baby chimp behaved himself quite well. He sat drinking milk from his wooden bottle and helped himself with the sponge algae cake lying on the table. He came and gave Iora a friendly tug. Iora had an abiding fascination for animals but the problem in her mind was overpowering at this instant.

"Actually . . . uh . . . I hope you had a good trip," said Iora awkwardly.

"It's alright, Iora. You can go ahead and ask me what you want to. We'll discuss my trip later," said Hoatzin.

Iora barely paused after that. She finished with, "Is it possible that it was not a dream?" taking a long breath.

Hoatzin didn't answer her; she was lost in thought. Iora was used to seeing her like that.

"Care to have some bat milk? I've got it from the

jungle," she finally asked Iora, breaking the silence.

"No, thank you. After seeing . . . or imagining that bat-like fish, I've lost all appetite for bat milk. Please tell me what you think of my dream . . ."

After a minute's silence, Hoatzin said softly, "I once dreamt of a faraway land. And I opened my eyes to see that I was born."

"I don't understand . . ."

"Never mind," said Hoatzin. "Reality is as dependent on dreams as dreams are dependent on reality. You will find your answer at the meeting of the Five."

"Five what?"

Hoatzin looked intently at her, or rather through her and said, "You can come in, Owlus."

Owlus opened the door, grinning. "How did you know I was outside? I was about to knock, you see."

"Let's say I heard some misplaced sound," said Hoatzin. "I suppose you're here for Iora."

"Not for her. But yeah, she has been acting funny, you know, since she was bitten by that worm. I've been trying to figure out what she's up to," said Owlus, casting a sideways glance at Iora.

"You've been following me around? Some people have exceptionally long noses!"

"We were discussing about dreams, Owlus, if that interests you," said Hoatzin.

"How dull! But well . . . what do you expect from Iora?" Owlus shrugged his shoulders.

Iora was about to reply when they heard a commotion and came out.

Kookaburra and Toucan had broken into a fight and even their family birds were fighting their feathers away.

"What's wrong with you two?" Hoatzin forced herself between them.

"I'll tell you what's wrong!" said Kookaburra, who had been completely overpowered by Toucan and now stood huffing, puffing and scratching his beard. "This con came to me yesterday and told me that on his jungle trip he had overheard two Amazons discuss an attack on Twitterland. But the only way they could be defeated was, they said, if someone called Kookaburra meditated on a treetop. He pleaded I do that and I've been meditating since morning. Then this guy brings Twitters telling them that I've gone mad and wouldn't come down the tree. And everyone starts pulling me down!"

Toucan laughed hysterically and Kookaburra fumed with rage. Hoatzin got busy sorting this out when Grandpa Cockatoo came looking for Iora.

"Come home and finish breakfast. Don't make your old grandpa run after you. You've got to take your medicine as well!"

Looking at the scene, Iora knew Hoatzin wouldn't be free anytime soon. She went along with Grandpa, her mind totally absorbed in what Hoatzin had said. Cockatoo glanced at Kookaburra, shook his head and went away.

The medicine was sleep-inducing and Iora slept through the afternoon. By the time she woke up, the coffee time rain was over and the sun was about to set. A hundred questions swirled in her mind and she started towards Hoatzin's cottage. Though curious, she was not worried as before. At least now she knew Hoatzin was here to help.

"Where do you think you are going?" asked the freshly trimmed shrub in front of Hoatzin's cottage.

"To meet Hoatzin . . . what else, pokey nose," she answered.

The bush moved its leaves and rustled, "She has left for another jungle trip."

7
The Quest of the Five

"What! But she just got back last night! Is she coming back soon?" shouted Iora.

"I am clueless," said the shrub, folding its leaves dismissively, no longer in the mood to talk.

Iora went home, disappointed and confused.

The next night, she sat all alone on the lakeshore, throwing small stones aimed at the sleeping water lilies. Iora had not been able to figure out anything the whole day. The night air was sweet with the fragrance of evening orchids. The moon was a thin arc suspended in a cloudy sky. "Iora . . ." a soft voice made her turn around to see Beetle Agogwe approaching.

"You're back so soon!" exclaimed Iora.

"I was headed to trade with Pebbles when one of the family birds told me you were bitten by a Rogue Thorn Worm. Now that is nasty. You've been getting in a lot of trouble lately. But by the time I come, your troubles are over," said Beetle.

"The trouble is not yet over for me, Beetle. Far from over," Iora sighed. She told him all that had happened. "After speaking to Hoatzin, I am sure that it was more than a dream. If only I could talk to her... Why did she leave so suddenly? My father . . . I hope he's not in danger."

"It is very strange indeed. It could have been a Ghost of Yellow Leaves near your well. They are known to be the agents of dark magic and are viler than even the Head Hunter tribe. It is said that they are the dead who find their way to the underworld from their graves. They need sacrifices of various creatures, and that too the best amongst each tribe and race, to keep living their undead lives." Beetle shuddered at the thought.

"I know. Madame Flameback told me that they hold up the limbs of the victim and remove various organs one by one. What if they really need Father for sacrifice? Grandpa and the others don't understand. It was not a dream!"

"Don't worry, my dear. We'll do something about it . . ."

"I've decided to leave tomorrow night," said Iora firmly.

"Leave for where? Heron has gone to the Wacky Wilderness and you can't go there! You don't have the training for it and you are not even friends with the resident creatures."

"There is no way I can get to Father on time. Grandpa says it is easier to find a squirrel's whisker in the river, than Father in the jungle. The safer bet is to find the meeting of Five, the one Hoatzin mentioned," said Iora. "What can it be?"

Beetle thought aloud, "Sounds familiar, meeting of five . . . five . . . five . . . Oh yes! I think she was talking about the meeting of the five rivers. They fall from the five hills into the Silver Lake! Perhaps you'll get your answers there. But then, that too is in the Wacky Wilderness . . ."

"So I have no choice but to go there. Alone."

"That is outrageous! Have you any idea how dangerous that place is? So many Twitters have lost their lives there that they call some areas The Twitters' Grave. It hides monstrous creatures; though I must say not all of them are wicked. There are even some naive-looking small ones, whose breath alone can kill you. Wandering spirits and forest ogres live in inaccessible caves. Their roars and cries can be heard in storms . . . Why don't you wait for Hoatzin to return?"

"I can't wait! Grandpa just refuses to listen and I can't sit doing nothing," she said getting up. "Tomorrow I leave. Hope no one has heard us." She looked at the sleeping trees, realising that the chirping crickets made it difficult to hear anything else.

Beetle tried in vain to persuade her and finally left with a whole lot of reluctance.

Iora spent the next day packing her little bag of

chameleon skin secretly with some potions and useful herbs. Chameleon skin things regained their brownish-pink colour after losing touch with living beings and this bag lay like a normal bag on Iora's bed. At night she retired early. Once all was still outside and inside, she left with her bag and a thin chameleon camouflage coverlet that covered her from head to toe.

She left a message on a small bark parchment for Grandpa, saying that she had to go on an inevitable mission and would return soon. It was a dark cloudy night. Her camouflage coverlet made her invisible to the night plants and animals. She reached the closed passage to the jungle. Water fell from a crystal orchid onto a crystal bowl, like the one at the entrance outside. She lifted the bowl gently with both hands and brought it up to the crystal orchid.

With a soft hum, the entrance opened and the jungle stretched before her, much darker than Twitterland. She removed the camouflage coverlet and stepped into the forest. The nightwalkers were out to forage for food on their set highways. Voices of the jungle meshed into the fabric of the night –a little quivering sound from near, a harsh yell from afar. Familiar with the surrounding jungle, Iora reached the bank of the Scar-faced River, where she'd seen the non-jungle dwellers. Her eyes slowly adjusted to the dim light that filtered in through the thick foliage above her.

"Excuse me, can anyone tell me the way to the

Silver Lake?" she asked a group of deer, grazing a little away from the river. All the animals stopped what they were doing and lifted their heads to look at her. No one answered, an alert and watchful look on their faces.

She was about to ask again when she was swept off her feet. She caught a glimpse of a dark figure jumping on the spot where she had just stood. It was a panther! It growled on missing its prey and the other animals fled at its sight.

Iora realised she was high above the ground on a big, flat branch with a strange-looking man by her side. A thin film of stretchable skin connected his forearms and legs forming membranous wings.

"Thank you very much for rescuing me. But I don't think I know who you . . ."

"He is my friend, Bara," came a voice from another branch.

"Beetle!"

"Hoo! I am glad I didn't come late this time for a change!" smiled Beetle, wiping sweat off his forehead. "What would I ever say to Heron if I let you go alone? The jungle is not as friendly as Twitterland. For herbivores you are a hunter and for carnivores a prey. Hardly any tree can speak or even understand Jungly. And, ah well, I do know a thing or two about the Wacky Wilderness."

"Thank you so much, Beetle!"

"Nah, it's nothing. Let's start for the Silver Lake now. Bara will guide us to the foot of one of the five hills.

“I’ll need to go home and inform my family first,” Bara said in a chirpy voice.

“Where is your home?” asked Iora.

“We’ll reach there by dawn,” said Bara, spreading his arms and flying further up from the platform towards the treetops. Beetle and Iora began climbing after him, meeting various animals in the many layers of the giant rainforest trees.

***

It was just before daybreak. Near the treetops it was quite bright, unlike the gloomy world below, where the nighttime mist had not yet lifted. An endless vista, much like a crumpled green mattress stretching in all the directions to the horizon, glistened in the fresh rays of the sun. This was the jungle canopy. Birds of prey swooped and soared and many other birds darted and hovered to get a morsel of food. Animals – mainly monkeys – moved about chattering, thousands of different insects sampled the nectar of blossoming flowers, and many more creatures like Bara flew above the treetops. Some big nests with sheltering roofs were scattered on the canopy, where winged children were perched.

“They are *Homo-avis*,” Beetle informed Iora. “They are mainly insect eaters; very shy but good friends once you know them. I bring them different roots and shoots from the ground.”

“Yes, Father once told me about them,” said Iora.

Bara went to one such nest and came back within moments. “I’ve informed my folks. Ready to go?”

“Yes, let’s do it,” said Beetle, taking Iora’s hand again.

Bara went flying ahead, stopping every few minutes to wait for them. They followed on the big branch ways, swayed on vines and hanging roots, and went up and down the tree canopy behind him. After travelling for three days, with only brief periods of rest, they reached the foothills of the Silver Lake.

“I’ve never come so far in the jungle before,” Iora told Beetle. She was very happy with herself.

After a warm thanks and farewell to Bara, they came down the forest floor, rested for some time, and ate some fruits and edible flowers. There was gurgling water nearby and they went in that direction. Iora reached a rock near the river and sat to drink. She realised that the water’s flow was upwards, not downwards! She was stunned to see the river curving and flowing uphill.

“Wow! How? What?”

“Don’t ask me all these questions, Iora. I’m not Hoatzin. This is the path we’ll be taking uphill. We’ve entered the Wacky Wilderness and the forest will get more and more enchanted now.”

After a long and tedious climb, they reached the top of the hill just before dusk.

The river fell down in a cascade into a large lake and there were four other hills from which four rivers cascaded down. One could smell water everywhere. The froth generated was so thick that it seemed a thousand clouds had gathered there.

"This is spectacular! I haven't seen anything like this in my life!" said Iora.

"I knew you'd feel that way. I travel far and wide, but this is my favourite place."

"It may sound strange, Beetle, but I feel I'm being watched constantly. I even felt someone's breath on my back once or twice," said Iora, looking around suspiciously.

"There is no one following us, Iora. Anyway, we have to trek down to reach the lake."

"No, Beetle, not now. I'm too tired and the sound of waterfall is like a lullaby . . ."

"Yes, little one, you should have some food and then get a good night's sleep. We'll start tomorrow morning when we're energetic again."

Beetle lit a small bonfire. After dinner, he climbed a tree and brought down large circular leaves, with which he quickly made two semi-circular tents for the night.

The next morning, they woke up refreshed and started downhill alongside the waterfall. It took them less time to come down than it had taken to climb up. Beetle showed her various new insects, roots and plants on the way and Iora learnt everything eagerly. But she could still feel someone following them. She kept looking back over her shoulders but there was no one. They reached the bottom of the hill in time for the coffee time rain. The lake seemed much bigger at close quarters. There was a little clearing and they sat down, listening to the sound of the falling water.

"Now what?" asked Iora.

"This is the meeting of the Five. I don't know how we can find your answers here. Let's start looking for signs in the forest after we rest for a while," said Beetle.

Just then, a mermaid emerged from the water on the bank near them. Resembling a pale dead fish, her bones protruded out of her upper body. She had long, pointed, zigzag teeth, deep sockets bearing yellow eyes and short spiky hair.

"Welcome friends . . . he! he! he!" she laughed in a thin piercing voice.

Beetle and Iora rose slowly. They moved backwards when she approached them, hurling herself forward with her two bony hands. Beetle saw a huge tilted tree whose thick roots covered a rock. Between the roots and the rock there was an opening. Just outside the opening lay small mud idols – all in the shape of snakes.

There was a terrifying rumble and the land beneath their feet began to shake. A chunk of land around the mermaid broke and went down the lake. The horrible shrieks of the mermaid were drowned in the roar.

"Earthquake!" shouted Beetle, and gestured frantically to Iora to get inside that opening between the tree and the rock. They both jumped straight inside the opening. It was a small mouth to a broad cave, which led underground. It was lit up with lamps, and a faint sound of flute came from below.

"Perhaps you'll find the answers here," said Beetle, half-happy, half-baffled and still shaking. They both went down the cave.

The tremors of the earthquake became lesser and lesser and finally everything became quite still, except for the music. After walking down for a while they reached a vast flat land, which was no less lovely than the rainforest above. There were waterfalls, mosses and ferns of various shapes, large transparent rocks carved in shapes of trees, and stones forming umbrella-shaped houses. Numerous effervescent liquids, placed in stone jars, brightly lit up the underground city. All kinds of snakes slithered around and hung from different places. Thin, but good-looking, yellow-skinned people moved about and smiled at each other perpetually, wearing clothes of discarded snake skin. A little, yellow-skinned boy played the flute below a snake idol.

"Interesssssting . . . Who would you be?" hissed a large, yellow-striped snake just above their heads, its flickering tongue touching their hair. Beetle almost lost his voice seeing it.

"I am Iora and this is Beetle, but who are you and who are these people?" answered Iora bravely.

The snake hissed, coiling around Beetle, "You musssst have heard about the Ghossssts of Yellow Leavessss."

8
The Ghosts of Yellow Leaves

Beetle nearly fainted and would have fallen to the ground if he were not in the snake's coil. Iora stood there, stunned, staring into the snake's eyes. The people moving about stopped smiling and the boy put his flute down.

"What are you doing here?" the snake snapped at Iora.

"I have come to save my father from your clutches! I can't fight you, so I offer myself as the sacrifice instead of my father," she said, going red in the face.

"Well, in that case I'll accept you as the ssssacrifice," said the snake, easing its grip around Beetle and approaching Iora.

"Sir, this is no joke," said an elderly man coming forward.

"Such a spoil sssport you are, Vipero, denying an old

snake an eassssy meal," frowned the snake, slithering away from the group.

Beetle still stood rooted to the same spot.

"What is the matter, child? What are you talking about and what are you doing here?"

"Are you really the Ghosts of Yellow Leaves?" Iora asked, adjusting her camouflage bag.

"Yes, that's what the jungle people call us. But we just call ourselves The People."

"Oh, well . . . I don't know if you're the same people I've heard about . . ." said Iora.

She didn't feel afraid of these strange people and felt it was best to tell them the truth. All the people and snakes gathered around her as she narrated the series of happenings, sitting on an emerald seat with Beetle by her side.

After she finished, Vipero said, "We have nothing to do with what you've told us. But I am not surprised that we've been linked again with such a story."

"Who are you then?" asked Iora.

"We are very much alive and not 'the buried dead', as other jungle people like to call us. From the beginning of time, we had inhabited the jungles above. Until one morning after the moonless night, around seventy sun years back, some young men of our tribe went to gather white leaves around the Silver Lake. They witnessed something appalling – twisted bodies of two of our fellow People. One of them was already dead and the other was gasping his last breaths. It seemed the lake had frozen the night before and was thawing then. The trees around which stood dried now seemed to be reviving. The last words of the other one before he died were, "That young Twitter Cooo . . ."

Mysteriously, the day after this incident, rumours floated around the forest that we were involved in invoking the dark forces. Everyone started suspecting our skin colour, which resembled yellow leaves. It became difficult for us to live in the jungle. All creatures, plants and tribes turned hostile towards us. Amazons started targeting and killing us, Agogwes let loose poisonous insects on us, Head Hunters made at least one trophy every day out of our people's heads . . .

Finally, we went to the Animal Angel. He handed us to the Guardianship of the Snakes. The snakes have been our friends ever since and they've allowed us to build our city in their own homes underground."

"I am shocked to hear all this," said Iora.

"So am I!" said Beetle, who had found his voice again. "But what had happened to the two Ghosts of Yello . . . I mean the two People and the lake?"

"He cannot ansssswer, because he does not know," said an old snake.

He was heavily wrinkled and he smiled at them; it made his face look like a crumpled, half-dead leaf. "Only the five jungle Angelssss can do these people justice by clearing their name . . ." he said. "I've known them for more than a century and there is not a more docile race in the entire wilder lands."

"What did you say?" said Iora, jumping to her feet.

"That they are the most docile . . ."

"No, not that. There are five forest Angels! Of course . . . It must have been the meeting of the Five Angels that Hoatzin had mentioned! I don't know if they can meet at all . . ."

"If the Five Angels come together, they can desssstroy all the dark forces of the forest. I am not sure, but perhaps dark forces are at work again," hissed the old snake, sneezing.

"Then I must meet them before the next moonless night when someone has plotted to kill Father. But where can I find them?"

"It is not an easy task, little Twitter. The meeting of the Five is perhaps jusssst a legend," said the snake, looking at the size of Iora and Beetle.

"But I will try. They are Angels after all. Why wouldn't they listen to the inhabitants of their own forest?"

"Well in that case . . . we only know where the Animal Angel resides and can give you directionssss," said the old snake sceptically. "But you should start tomorrow and be our guestssss for tonight."

The boy resumed playing the flute and was joined by a girl with crystals full of water, which she tinkled with two crab claws.

"Let's hear some poetry!" said a voice, and everyone

turned to a green snake with white dots and beady yellow eyes.

"Well if you insisssst," he said with a cloudy look on his flat face. Silence fell and Iora and Beetle looked on.

The snake began singing in a misty voice, as the little boy and girl played music,

"I'm just a chapter of loathing
In the naïve human book
Ssslimy, ssslithery, sssneaky, creepy
With fangsss and ugly look

♫♩♫

I give them a squeeze of dread
When I'm just hanging on a tree
And when I bask in the grassss
They dash away from me

♩♫♩

Or chase me with a cudgel
Or empty acid in my home
Or beat my brethren to pulp
Till their blameless sssoul is gone

♫♩♫

If they find our discarded ssskin
They'll keep it in their vaults
As it is thought to bring riches
And purge them of their faults

♩♫♩

Else they inscribe me as evil
Make appalling shows on me
When I just want to be left
On a sheet of obsssscurity

♫♩♪♫

I do not carry a club or fire
Neither walk six feet tall
Nor keep humans' skin for luck
Nor chase and bite them all

♩♪♫♩♪

So many times I spot them
When they are unaware
I prefer to go unobserved
Before I'm greeted with a ssscare"

♫♩♪♫♫♩♪♫♩♪

"Hear, hear!" shouted The People. "Well said!" praised some.

Dinner was served near a stream. Beetle could hardly swallow the earthworm soup or the fly-eye custard. But what he found the most difficult to eat was the dung beetle pudding! Still not convinced of the Ghosts of Yellow Leaves' story, he didn't have the courage to refuse to eat.

Next morning, Beetle received the directions to reach the Animal Angel. Beetle and Iora came out of the underground city to the lake by the same tunnel. A large piece of the bank had been washed away by the previous evening's earthquake but some grass had already sprouted on the bare broken ground. Beetle was tired of memorising the complex directions so he plucked a large, velvety Drawing Leaf from a bush and pressed his finger to draw the directions – "Right from the Spooky Stream, down the Formidable Falls, opposite the Singing Sticks . . ." The leaf left purple marks wherever his finger pressed, making a rough map.

***

A little while later, Iora was walking by the side of a stream. The jungle plants and vines dripped and drooped from either side.

"Which Twitter could it possibly be, who betrayed the jungle seventy years back? Who is the elder Twitter whose name starts with 'Cooo'?"

Just then, she heard a faint growl. "What is that sound?" she whispered.

"That," Beetle smiled and said, "is my stomach. All that dung beetle pudding! Yuck! Will you wait for five minutes here? I will just freshen up and come." And with that Beetle disappeared behind some bushes. Iora sat on a rock, trying to speak to some very unfriendly bees who just wouldn't respond.

"Shhh . . . you dere . . ." came a grumpy voice.

Iora turned around and almost touched two very big mossy eyes, each the size of her head. It was a huge chameleon with three horns protruding out of its head. She got up hurriedly, almost falling, as she took a couple of steps back.

“You are de lucky one to be feasting her eyes upon my great hart,” it said peevishly.

“Your great heart?” asked Iora.

“Hart . . . hart . . . you illiterate! The one that I’ve made!”

“You mean Art,” said Iora, squinting her eyes.

“Yes, one which I’ve made outh of insects’ whings. Just follow me up the tree if you want to see it,” ordered the strange chameleon.

“Thank you. But I can’t come. I’m waiting for a friend,” replied Iora.

The chameleon unfurled its long fleshy tongue that lay rolled up in its mouth and shot it towards Iora. She ducked behind a rock and slowly raised her head to see a large transparent bee, which had all its insides clearly visible through its transparent skin, in the chameleon’s mouth.

“It was hovering righth behind you,” said the chameleon, as it swallowed the bee in one giant slurp.

“So whath were you saying?”

“Uh . . . nothing,” said Iora.

“Follow me up, up, up,” it said, climbing the tree.

Iora had no choice but to follow the chameleon. She climbed after it. She had barely risen a little from the ground when she heard a roaring warning advancing towards her. “Out of the way! Out of the way!”

Within a minute, hundreds of wild boars, black as night, with eight long curved tusks on their snouts came rushing forward. They went along crushing everything that came in their way.

"Out of the way . . ." the noise decreased and vanished once they were out of sight.

"Iora! Iora!" Beetle called from behind the trees.

"I'm up here," she answered, climbing down.

"Thank the Multi-legged Angel!" sighed Beetle.

"Let's get out of here fast!" said Iora, looking up the huge tree where she could see the chameleon climbing high up, muttering to itself.

"Don't worry, those wild hogs wouldn't return. Poor creatures find themselves at a loss during the daytime," said Beetle, looking at the trampled vegetation.

"Not them. IT!" she said, pointing upward.

One look at the huge chameleon and Beetle just grabbed at Iora's hand and rushed away.

Beetle was a little familiar with this part of the jungle but their pace was slowed due to his upset stomach. They could not move on the canopy or middle layers of the forest trees and this made their progress slower.

"Oh my beautiful tummy has flattened so much," Beetle kept complaining. Finally, the next day, he found the spear-shaped Smudgestopper flowers to treat his stomach. They hung on a vine in the middle tier of a tree. Beetle spotted a troupe of lion monkeys gathered near the flowers and climbed slowly up, making sure they didn't catch him.

These monkeys had a mane around their faces and a

bushy tip of the tail. The leader of the troupe wore a leafy turban and held a staff in one of his hands. His wife and children sat at his back and four lieutenant monkeys sat on his right and left. The assembly of monkeys threw food at the king and his family and they ate it. Beetle came silently and plucked the flowers. But just when he began climbing down, a monkey spotted him.

"Look at this shorty here, trying to steal our flowers!" he shouted.

All the monkeys gathered around Beetle, who stood on a stretched branch holding the flowers in a tiny little leaf pouch.

He apologised and said, "Just for my stomach, friends." The monkeys really had no use whatsoever of the flowers.

"Shorty has an upset stomach," shouted a monkey and they all giggled. Beetle was not ruffled and joined in their jokes. Finally, the king finished his meal, rose and came with the help of his staff and poked his long finger in Beetle's nostrils.

"Leader wants you to entertain us," explained one of the monkeys.

Beetle knew there was no sense in arguing. Agogwes were one cheerful tribe and would sing and dance every day. He began singing and dancing on the flat branch,

"A sad, long-haired boy
Was so devoid of joy
Why did he have such long hair?
Was he half-human half-bear?
The boy would sit alone and weep
Until he would fall asleep

He tried to cut his hair short
But it grew in layers and lot
Until it touched his knee bone
As if it had a mind of its own
The boy became coy and meek
For all treated him like a freak

He was just a laughing stock
Until one day on a long walk
He met a four-tailed hare
Who was proud, as he was rare
The boy sat down and thought
Was he too rare or what?

Now he plaited his hair in braids
And used them as extra aides
Carrying four pots instead of two
And flaunted to give all a good view
The boy moved with clenched jaw
As everyone held him in awe

Now the long-haired boy was sought
By his neighbours and the whole lot
"With such gift he is bestowed!
In half time he carries dual load!"
The boy's life became full of laughter
And he lived happily ever after"

Beetle finished but all the monkeys stood there staring at him. Their leader approached Beetle again, turned around, slapped him with his tail, and went and sat down on the branch. All the monkeys hooted.

"Can I go now?" Beetle asked sceptically. The leader nodded. Beetle climbed down as fast as possible and joined Iora, who had been watching everything from a little distance.

Beetle felt much better after eating the Smudgestopper flowers. They stopped for a while during the coffee time rain and just before dusk, reached the spot where the Sleepy Treepy was supposed to be.

"I don't have any clue of the forest past this area." Beetle looked around and glanced at his Drawing Leaf. "The directions are only till this spot."

"Now where can this Sleepy Treepy be?" said Iora, and looked up and down the lush vegetation.

"Quiet!" whispered Beetle.

Along with the babble of some monkeys, chirrups from birds and gurgles from the stream, a regular snoring sound boomed out from beyond a small brook on their left. They crossed the brook and went in the direction of the sound, which was getting louder and louder with every step. The evening got darker and Beetle lit a torch. A few paces away, they saw a distinct stout tree with a broad trunk and a tuft of pinkish-grey leaves with brown roots hanging from it. The sound originated from this tree.

"Excuse me," said Iora, "are you Sir Sleepy Treepy?" But there was no response.

"Excuse me, Sir," it was now Beetle who came forward. Still no response!

They waited for almost half an hour and then, finally, shouted to wake the tree up. His snoring had increased to a rattling noise when Iora went up to him and pulled his roots hard.

With a snort, the tree slowly opened his woody eyes, which were on his trunk, and straightened his tuft of leaves. "Is it morning already?" he blurted in a grating voice, his mouth placed right in the middle of his tuft of leaves.

"It is night," said Iora.

"So why did I get up?" he said, half-closing his woody eyes again.

"No, no, no, no . . . wait!" shouted Beetle. "We need your help. The Ghosts of Yellow Leaves have sent us. They said you could direct us to the Animal Angel."

"Oh yes, nice people . . . those Ghosts . . ." said the tree, dozing off again.

"Sir Sleepy Treepy! We need help with directions!"

shouted Iora, shaking him up with all her strength.

"Oh yes, directions. What directions?" replied the tree, still in a complete daze.

"Aargh! This is too much!" exclaimed Iora.

"Ghosts of Yellow Leaves . . . directions to the Animal Angel . . . remember?" said Beetle.

"Yes, yes, you just go in the direction of my ears . . ."

"But where are your ears?" asked Iora.

"Why, where else can they be? Right here at the back of my eyes, the other side of the trunk," said the tree, looking rather hurt. Then he continued in a drowsy voice, "In a straight line, fifty-three trees away, there is the Leech Lake. You've to cross that. On the other side where you'll see . . ." he again started slumbering when Iora pulled his roots.

"Where was I? Yes . . . the Leech Lake. Cross it and there you'll find the pink elephant. Go in the direction of its tail and you'll reach the Petrified Pond. There you'll find the Animal Angel. Now can I go back to sleep?" asked the tree, its leaves drooping.

"Thank you very much, Sir," said Beetle, but the tree was fast asleep by then.

"We'll spend the night here and resume in the morning," said Beetle, plucking some leaves and making two small circular huts for the night.

The next morning, they started before the first rays of sun had penetrated the thick jungle canopy. The night-time vapour pall had not lifted and the forest was like a sauna. It buzzed with animal activity in the early morning hours. The morning animals, in the early hours, are usually half-asleep and dim-witted, unlike the alert night animals. A fat monkey came and sat next to Beetle and looked at him while they had their breakfast. He kept moving his head quickly to see Beetle and what he ate in turns. Beetle didn't mind it sitting next to him even when it started to pull his beard wrapped around his waist. He lost his temper and chased it with a stick when the monkey bit him hard, failing to loosen his tightly draped beard.

They counted fifty-three trees and reached a steep gap running deep down the ground. There was a frail bridge made out of hanging lianas.

"I guess we have to cross this," said Beetle, "but it seems very frail and has lots of gaps. You'll have to follow close behind me."

"Don't worry, I'll be fine. Father has taught me to walk on liana bridges."

"Then let's do it," said Beetle, setting foot on the bridge. He shrieked and fell back on the ground.

"What's wrong?" asked Iora, running towards him.

She caught a glimpse of what Beetle had seen and yelped. Just below the bridge, the precipice was filled with gigantic leeches standing in their customary U-shaped curve, occasionally standing upright and lifting their sucking mouths towards the bridge.

"How are we supposed to cross this, Beetle?"

"We'll have to dare it, Iora. There is no other way to reach the Angel."

"Well, in that case, let's do it," said Iora, coming forward.

"Now wait! I'll go first and you come behind. It is just a small bridge . . . we can cross it. As such their mouths are not really reaching the bridge." Beetle set his foot on the bridge. He slowly advanced, balancing himself, one step at a time. The bridge swayed gently and he could clearly hear the slushy sounds coming out of the leeches' gaping mouths. There were no eyes, no ears, nothing but mouths on the black bent slimy bodies.

Iora followed him placing her feet prudently. They were about to reach the other end when a leech straightened itself and its mouth reached just below Beetle. Because of the suddenness, Beetle lost balance and slipped.

He managed to catch a liana hanging loosely below the bridge. Iora reached forward and caught his hand. By now the bridge had started shaking violently and before she could pull him up, she also lost balance and slipped, managing to hold another hanging liana. The leeches had detected movement and food. They piled below them, stretching and trying hard to reach the dangling bodies.

Beetle reached out to Iora to throw her back on the bridge but he only made it worse for himself. Iora's grip loosened.

"Owlus!" cried Beetle looking at Iora.

"What? You're thinking of Owlus? The last person to think of at this time!" she said, struggling to avoid leeches' mouths which almost touched their legs.

"You Fat Incredible Twitter!" came a voice from above them.

Iora looked up and gaped in shock, as Owlus looked down at her from the liana bridge.

9
An Unexpected Rendezvous

"What on earth are you doing here!" exclaimed Iora. Owlus reached out his hand and she was on the bridge in a couple of minutes. They both held Beetle's arms and pulled him up as well. Beetle and Iora looked at each other and then at Owlus in shock mixed with relief. They could not utter a word as the leeches gathered below in a huddle stretched their elongated bodies to reach them. The three of them waited for the bridge to become steady and inched towards the other end.

Still shaking, they moved away from the crevice and sat down in a heap below a tree.

"Now will someone tell me what's going on?" asked Iora.

"My ears are waiting too," said Beetle. They both looked towards Owlus lying flat on the moss.

"I've not been getting the right education! No one

warned me that people are going to be ungrateful when I save their lives!" said Owlus.

"Cut it out, Owlus, and explain!" said Iora.

"Do you think that everyone is blind to your tomfoolery? I, for one, am not!" retorted Owlus.

"And who are you, my granddad?" Iora shouted.

"Someone should tell both of you to reduce those fat chunks! Such a hard time I had pulling you up!" continued Owlus, ignoring Iora's questions.

"Don't fight like babies!" said Beetle in his shrill voice and came between Owlus and Iora who were about to pounce on each other.

"Now tell me, Owlus, What, Why and How?" he said in a calm tone.

"It seems you're not as terrifying as the kids make you to be, little fellow, and they give credit to Iora for making friends with so called abominable people!" Owlus scowled.

"To the point, Owlus," said Beetle.

"Yeah, well, I'd been watching Iora behave weirdly after being bitten by the Rogue Thorn Worm. I followed her around Twitterland and when I was about to call it off, I heard the conversation between you two. At once I decided to follow her in the jungle."

"Some people just can't mind their own business. Didn't I tell you, Beetle, I felt someone was following us?"

"Iora, I'll listen to you later. Yes, then what, Owlus?"

"I covered myself from head to toe in my father's robe

of Chameleon Skin and followed her out of Twitterland. I left a note on Barking Bark set to bark next morning to inform my parents about my outing with Iora. I managed to eat, sleep and walk following you at a distance. In fact, I was the one who slipped first through the gateway to the underground city of the Ghosts of Yellow Leaves. My camouflage robe tore a little when I tried to run away from the passing wild forest hogs. I had to hide behind the trees while following you after that. When I saw both of you hanging on the bridge, I had no choice but to throw away my torn camouflage robe and rescue you."

"Why do you say you didn't have a choice, Owlus? You could have let us be sucked by the leeches," said Iora grumpily.

"What! And be lost in the jungle forever? How would I get back if you became food to those slimy hoses? I never knew this outing would become so crazy!" said Owlus, angrily pushing his straight hair off his eyes.

"Whatever be his motivation, Iora, we must thank Owlus for saving our lives. And since we are stuck together, it would be better to carry on as friends," concluded Beetle, closing this issue. Without waiting for response he went on, "We don't have a lot of time before the next moonless night with a mammoth task in hand. I can't imagine how terrified your families must be for both of you, but there is no turning back now. Let us search for the elephant. We should be able to spot it easily."

“Now since we can’t get rid of you, Owlus, you better start looking in that direction. I will go in this,” said Iora and ran away behind the trees.

Owlus frowned and started probing. They searched and searched but got no trace of any elephant. Finally, they gathered at the same place.

“What is this terrible smell?” said Owlus, wrinkling his nose.

“Oh, that’s nothing,” said Beetle.

“What do you mean nothing? This place is stinking awfully!” insisted Owlus; Iora wriggled her nose too.

“Oh well, you know the dung beetles didn’t do my stomach much good . . . Another dose of Smudgestopper flowers and I’ll be fine,” said Beetle, embarrassed as Owlus looked at him with disgust.

“I should find the flowers here. Meanwhile, you both eat something and then we’ll start again. There are some citrus fruits growing on these trees,” said Beetle, pointing upwards.

Fortunately, Beetle located Smudgestopper flowers, after which the trio climbed up different trees and devoured the citrus fruits.

“Hey, there is a bunch of Munchy Mushrooms growing inside this tree!” shouted Iora, standing midway on a branch, where an opening led inside the hollow trunk.

Some pink mushrooms could be seen on the other side of the hollow interior. They were out of reach but too tempting to leave. Iora was in an awkward position, stretching her hand inside the trunk, when some swaying leaves tickled her feet and she lost balance. With a shriek echoing through the dark walls, Iora could feel her body falling freely. Instinctively, acting according to the training given by her father, she tried to position herself in a certain posture to minimise the impact when she touched the ground.

Beetle and Owlus came running in through a small opening at the bottom that led to the void insides of the tree trunk.

“Iora! Iora! Are you okay?” said Beetle breathlessly.

“Oh yes, haven’t laid down on such a soft bed after leaving Twitterland,” came Iora’s voice from a little elevation. Beetle immediately took out two stones from his bag and lit a torch on a small twig. It lighted up the dark insides of the trunk. The inner walls were dotted with pink mushrooms and in the middle of the trunk stood a pink elephant shaped out of a cluster of burgeoning mushrooms. At the top of the elephant’s back Iora stretched her limbs.

“Wow!” said Iora and Owlus, both at the same time.

Though Iora knew she’d landed on soft ground, she didn’t know it was a large mushroom elephant. While climbing down, she saw something moving behind the elephant.

“I saw something . . . let’s go at the back.”

In the light of the torch they saw the elephant’s tail

moving up and down due to the mushrooms growing and un-growing at a fast pace repeatedly.

"This is the direction we've to follow," said Iora.

"Yeah, that's right," said Beetle.

They came out and went that way.

As they proceeded, the general noises of the jungle diminished and a silence descended upon the surroundings. The normal thick vegetation blocking the sun became thicker and made the forest floor darker. The silence was so complete that their own footsteps made loud thuds. After walking a little ahead, it became pitch dark and they could hardly move forward without bumping into trees and each other. Beetle fumbled in his pockets, removed his firestones and slow burning twigs, and lighted a small fire.

"Stop!" whispered Owlus, as soon as the torch was lit.

Beetle and Iora looked around to see dozens of fiery eyes gleaming like embers in the trees above, staring at them. Beetle held his torch high and looked at the burning eyes scattered above. There came along a droning sound and the eyes seemed to be moving now. With a soft thump, something landed near them and Beetle brought down the torch to see what it was. A creature resembling a panther, with two pairs of translucent wings and a sharp horn coming out from the middle of its head, crouched in front . . . ready to attack.

10
The Animal Angel

"You who dare! Speak of your purpose or die!" droned the creature, its wings now folded on its sides.

"We are here to see the Animal Angel," replied Iora.

"Indeed . . . Purpose?" it droned.

"Can't the followers come to see the Angel?" said Iora steadily, trying not to look at its sharp auburn horn. "Why are you blocking our way?"

The creature rubbed its paws on the ground and droned aloud. Similar creatures came flying down from the trees. "We have a blabbermouth amongst us today, don't we? Purpose!" it droned again, fiercely this time.

Beetle quickly spoke before Iora could and explained in brief.

"Our Animal Angel has been expecting some visitors, but I didn't know it would be such a weird lot," it looked at them unconvinced, and reluctantly said, "Carry on!"

Beetle, Iora and Owlus resumed their journey, happy to leave those glinting eyes behind.

"Look who was calling us 'weird creatures'! The nerves they have!" grumbled Owlus.

"Why didn't you express your views to them?" asked Iora.

The darkness decreased but the silence remained. Gradually, they came to an open patch where it was unusually bright. A little lake sparkled, illuminating the surrounding greenery. But there was something odd about it. Its waters were as still as the sky.

"Is it frozen?" asked Owlus.

Beetle went forward and touched it. He looked confused. Then he took out his firestones and rubbed them on it.

"It is a diamond," he said after deliberation.

"So this is the Petrified Pond!" exclaimed Iora, beholding it with wonder.

"Mind you, this is something that deserves to be called truly 'Incredible'," said Owlus, gazing sideways at Iora.

"Now what next?" mumbled Beetle.

"We should look around for clues," Iora suggested.

"This looking around for clues is getting on my nerves," growled Owlus.

"Why . . . because you can't find any?" snapped Iora, when a chubby white baby elephant appeared from behind the trees.

He had a little tuft of hair in the middle of his head. He stopped, smiled at them, untangled his hair with his trunk and said in a baby voice, "I am Emphuchi. You must be Iora, Beetle and Owlus."

"Yes, dear," said Beetle.

"The Animal Angel awaits you," said the elephant.

"But where to go, fatso?" asked Owlus.

"Oh sorry, will show you the way," Emphuchi answered as Iora frowned at Owlus.

The elephant strolled near a corner of the pond and pressed one of his feet on it. The opposite corner of the diamond began to rise vertically. There was an entrance to a cave underneath and Emphuchi told them to go inside. Iora stepped down with Beetle, followed by a hesitant Owlus.

"What are you doing?" yelled Owlus, standing at the cave entrance, to Emphuchi who was about to close the cave with the Petrified Pond.

"My work is done. I'm going to play," answered Emphuchi, adjusting his hair with his trunk.

"This is absurd! So now we're trapped in an underground cave by an insufferably cute, fat elephant. Makes me wonder, are you and him some distant relatives?" said Owlus, looking at Iora.

"Enough already!" cautioned Beetle.

They walked ahead in the dimly lit cave and reached a large space where the cave divided into many caves.

"Don't tell me!" exclaimed Owlus.

"We'll take different entrances."

"But there are more than a dozen entrances, which one to take . . ." said Beetle.

"Who's disturbing the peace of the Animal Angel?"

They saw a hefty proboscis monkey with an extra-large hanging nose, a red face and big potbelly, walking towards them on two feet. He munched on a twisted root. Just behind him a tiny, rosy-cheeked primate Slow Loris with very thin limbs, round face and glassy eyes, followed.

"You must be Iora and company," said the monkey, scrutinising all the three.

"Excuse me! I think you mean Owlus and company," said Owlus, not afraid of the large-nosed ape.

"No one asked for your opinion, Twitterboy, as no one asked you to follow Iora," said the monkey, calmly munching on the root.

Owlus was taken aback.

"How does he know this?" he whispered to Iora, and then fell silent.

"Follow me," said the monkey, going into a dark cave.

"Where are we going?" asked Iora.

"You will soon get to know everything, so be patient," replied the monkey and led the way with the tiny primate running behind.

After every few paces, more caves split from the one they entered and the proboscis monkey went ahead as though it was a well-marked path. It was an utterly confusing maze of passages and chambers. Though Owlus was tempted more than once to say something about finding the way back, he kept quiet.

After numerous caves and sub-caves, they reached a faintly lit stone antechamber with a high roof. Its walls were strewn with iridescent turquoise blue beads and a distant sound of gurgling water could be heard, though there was no water in sight. At the far corner of this antechamber stood a towering figure.

"My lord, Iora has arrived," said the monkey.

"Thank you, Proboscis Porty," said the figure, coming forward in the light.

There was an audible gasp by Iora, Beetle and Owlus. There stood in front of them a majestic creature, with the body of a jaguar and tail of an anaconda. Two curved teeth protruded out of his mouth and there were three horns on his back. Owlus was speechless and Beetle groped for words when Iora advanced towards him.

"The Animal Angel! I . . . We are . . . so . . . so . . . honoured to meet you!"

"So you recognise me," said the Angel, tenderly, in a voice quite dissimilar to his appearance. He had gentle eyes and on a closer look, Iora saw wrinkles all over his face and form.

"Yes, Angel. My father has described the Five Angels to me."

"Heron is a very prudent Twitter," said the Angel. "And I know why you've come here."

"Then please tell me what is going on and what can we do about it?"

Owlus and Beetle had also come by her side.

"Why don't you three sit down," said the Angel. "I tire quite easily nowadays."

They sat down a little away from him but the two monkeys kept standing.

"I can't give you all the answers; neither can I tell you what to do. All I can do is show you the path. You are the one who has to choose and decide."

"What is the path, my Angel?"

"The Five of us, we Five sentries of Nature, whom you call Angels, protect the jungle and balance its natural cycles and rhythms. But we too have cycles. Every few thousand sun years there comes a period when one of the Angles is the weakest. That is the time when the anti-natural forces, headed by its personified form – *Homo-diabolus*, gains power and tries to take control of the jungle rhythms to become invincible. But he can't gain control on all the Angels together. He has to overtake the Angels one by one. And he starts with the weakest link, which is me this time. So the Five Angels have to come together to ward the dark anti-natural forces," said the Animal Angel, swaying his heavy snake tail.

"But, Angel, who are these anti-natural forces? Are they the Ghosts of Yellow Leaves?" asked Owlus, who had somewhat regained his confidence.

"No, Owlus. Evil is never race specific. The Ghosts of

Yellow Leaves have been victimised. Seventy years back, the Bird Angel was completing her cycle and was very weak. *Homo-diabolus* tried to take control of the natural rhythms when two brave Ghosts of Yellow Leaves tried to stop him. And they succeeded. However, they died in the endeavour. Though they'd united the Five Angels, they failed to find the sixth element of the jungle – its Spirit."

"Sixth element?" all the three said in surprise.

"We've never heard of it," said Beetle.

"Yes, not many know about it. The Spirit of the Jungle is not an Angel and has no followers. But it is symbolic – representing life."

"That means I'm going to die if we don't find this sixth element? Please also show us the path back home, when you're showing the path ahead!" cried Owlus.

"Yes, it is not for the faint-hearted people, only for the bravest of brave," said Proboscis Porty to whom the little primate had just handed a green twig to chew.

"Faint-hearted! You must be talking about Iora. I was asking the path back home for her, just in case," said Owlus, blushing a little.

"Yeah, right!" Iora exclaimed.

"Now is *not* the time!" said Beetle in an undertone.

"This time I am the one who is completing the cycle," sighed the Angel, tiredly. "I will regain my strength and powers after this moonless night. But on the moonless night, I will be the weakest. Mind you, this is the longest moonless night of the year. The sinister forces will get the most powerful this night and will try to overcome the jungle Angels. Their chances are very strong."

"But who wants my father's blood?" asked Iora, who couldn't hold back the question any longer.

"Must be one of the staunchest followers of the anti-natural forces. It is possible they may be the same followers who tried seventy years back when their attempts were foiled. They may come back with power manifold this time. They've got a second chance – it has happened after ages that two Angels have completed their cycle within hundred years. They may need Heron's blood to achieve their final goal. And as to why, well, that is for you to find out, my dear."

"My Angel, how can this be prevented?" asked Beetle.

"Meeting of the Five Angels on the moonless night, with the sixth element – the Spirit of the Jungle."

"But where and how can you all meet?" asked Iora.

"Find all the Angels and tell them to come to one pre-decided place near a water source on the moonless night. The two brave People, Ghosts of Yellow Leaves as you call them, had requested us to come near the Silver Lake. So where would you like us to meet?"

They looked clueless but eventually Iora said, "We would be honoured to have the Angels come to the bank of the Scar-faced River near Twitterland."

"Then Twitterland it shall be," said the Angel, rising.

"Where shall we go now?" asked Beetle hastily.

"The Insect Angel would be the nearest. Proboscis Porty will give you the directions," said the Angel, turning towards the fat-nosed monkey. "From thereon you can ask directions from each Angel to the next one."

"But you didn't tell us where we'll find the sixth element – the Spirit?" asked Beetle.

"Nature designates a different Spirit every few years. It can be a wild flower, a bush baby, a millipede or a jaguar. Keep your senses alert. But most of all, keep your hearts open and you'll find it. And remember, you only have seventeen days to go before the moonless night. Not a very long time, I would say." The Angel turned to go out of the antechamber.

"Forgive me, Angel, I can't help but ask," said Iora, "if the Angels know they've to meet every time one Angel completes the cycle to preserve the jungle life, why don't they meet themselves?"

The Animal Angel smiled for the first time. "Angels can guide. But the fight for survival has to be fought by the creatures themselves. That's the law of nature."

11
The Suspicious Twitter

Paying respects to the Angel, the trio followed the two monkeys in the maze of caves again. Proboscis Porty ate perpetually and the little primate, Slow Loris, would disappear in some cave now and then to re-emerge with more food for Proboscis to eat.

"I hope we don't meet the revolting flying leopards or the freeloader leeches or some sugary sweet jumbo!" fussed Owlus.

"They all are there to guard the Animal Angel till he regains his powers. Better not upset them," said the munching Proboscis Porty.

"I wouldn't dare upset the fat jumbo . . . I can't imagine the consequences!"

The proboscis monkey looked at the sniggering Owlus but didn't say anything.

"Can I speak, please?" the primate, Slow Loris, asked

Proboscis Porty.

"Go ahead, Fast Loris," he answered, still munching.

"Why is this Slow Loris called *Fast* Loris?" whispered Owlus incredulously.

"Proboscis Porty only advices. He doesn't have to give explanations," started Fast Loris as soon as he got the chance to speak. "The little jumbo you are so amused about is the only one with the power and strength to open the Petrified Pond. The Leoparbees' stings can suck the dark soul out of anybody that carries one. The fact you crossed them is that none of you has one."

"Owlus with no dark soul!" Iora looked shocked.

"And," continued Fast Loris, "the Leechums don't eat you. You lie in their dark bellies alive until you rot and die of old age. They're living prisons."

Owlus turned white hearing this.

"But don't worry, you don't have to go the same way," Fast Loris said happily, observing Owlus's expression. "Proboscis Porty will explain you the way once you're out. He's a little busy eating now."

"And when is his lunch going to get over . . . at dinner time?" whispered Owlus, shaking his hair off his eyes.

Once Fast Loris started speaking there was no stopping.

"And Father says I should be called Babbler instead of Iora!" she mumbled.

"Now I know why he's called *Fast* Loris!" said Owlus.

"The Animal Angel takes care of the whole jungle and

this is our turn to take care of him. You know those blue beads covering the walls of his chamber are the frozen droplets of Astral Trickle, the divine rainfall. They possess celestial healing powers," said Fast Loris. No one replied but he didn't seem to notice. "Do you know what the Animal Angel's tail, horns and teeth do?"

"Never mind, we don't want to know," teased Owlus, who itched to find out.

"I knew you wouldn't know! With his roar he keeps the hunters and hunted, the grass eaters and flesh eaters under control. By the sweep of his tail he clears the forest and ensures that not a single leaf goes wasted. And with the three horns on his back he balances the volcanic powers under the earth. He is the Survival Instinct of the jungle! My ignorant friends, that is the Animal Angel for you – Survival Instinct with teeth!"

They'd reached the entrance of the cave below the Petrified Pond.

"Now if you are done," said Proboscis Porty.

"Yes, Porty, right away," said Fast Loris, and made a strange trumpeting sound.

Within moments, the diamond lifted vertically and Emphuchi was seen in a corner. "Welcome out again," he said, adjusting his tuft of hair.

"Now will you stop doing that! Nothing is going drastically wrong with your five strands of hair!" said Owlus irritably.

Emphuchi appeared hurt but Iora quickly said, "He is

kidding, Emphuchi. Look who's talking about adjusting his hair!"

Proboscis handed his halfeaten twig to Fast Loris. "Call the directions," he said.

"Shouldn't he say *bring* the directions?" Iora asked Beetle.

Fast Loris whistled. A bright blue butterfly came fluttering towards them and sat on the back of Proboscis Porty's palm.

"These are your directions," Proboscis told Beetle.

"I don't understand," he replied.

Proboscis brought the butterfly closer to them and said, "Meet Silver Sparks."

He gently stroked the edges of its blue wings and whispered a note. The butterfly took off and a silvery trail of sparks followed her flight making a glinting pattern in the air, which faded after a few moments. "This is the path to the Bird Angel from this point. You can take Silver Sparks along. She will not lead the way, nor warn you of perils, she'll only show the directions. But you need to communicate with her in Whistle-whisper."

"But we don't know that," said Beetle.

"Iora, I understand, is good with languages," said Proboscis Porty.

"How do you know that?" asked Iora.

Owlus frowned. "Yeah, I was told that truth crawls and falsehood flies. No wonder this false rumour has flown here in advance."

Proboscis continued speaking to Beetle. "There are only a few things which Iora needs to communicate with Silver Sparks. I'm sure she can learn this in no time.

Fast Loris taught Iora different whistling notes and Proboscis got busy eating again, looking for worms. The sun had gone down. The trio, who decided to spend the night nearby, bid farewell to the monkey duo, which went down the Petrified Pond.

The night had come to life with violence and the night animals were out on prowl. The jungle buzzed with activity – howl from near, a cry from afar, the constant chirping of crickets, the hiccupped croaks of frogs, a slithering sound below, a rustling sound above. After eating whatever they could gather, Beetle build three leaf huts for the night.

Iora said to Beetle, "It is not only about father anymore . . . it is about our jungle. We should try our best, shouldn't we?"

"Oh yes, little one, we'll see this through."

Iora lay awake listening to the canopy rustling with unseen life. Underneath, the nightwalkers were about but they were invisible in the darkness. Night whispered its lullaby and finally Iora drifted off to sleep.

They woke up to an unusually humid morning. The sun was shielded behind heavy clouds. A small animal of mongoose tribe approached Beetle and snuffed him curiously. Owlus enjoyed the sight.

"Ideally, it should take us three days to reach this

place," said Beetle, looking at the fading silvery directions Silver Sparks had displayed, "and if we maintain our pace, by evening we will enter the mountainous forest."

The trio picked up their small handbags and started on their onward journey. The sky was barely visible under the thick canopy. Light decreased further and they knew the sky would be overcast with low-lying clouds. Animal activity reduced to the minimum. Jets of hot air and menacing noises interrupted the still, oppressive atmosphere. A terrible roaring sound rolled away in the distance and a tremendous deluge followed. The sky began to empty its pitcher.

"Wrong time for this torrential rain!" sighed Beetle. "This is not the normal coffee time rain."

"I hope it stops soon," joined Iora, "I'm already drenched."

"You're telling me!" exclaimed Owlus, who had slipped in a pool of water.

Water started accumulating on the forest floor.

"It would be better if we walk in the middle layers of the forest," Beetle suggested, and they climbed a tree. After a little while, the forest floor was flooded.

Spending a wet night, the next day they dragged themselves to walk on the huge branch paths in the middle level of the trees, which was quite high above the ground. The branches were slippery and the rain beat everything in small whacks. Insects hid beneath leaves and crevices, birds silently sat on branches with furled feathers, snakes coiled on stems, and monkeys, jaguars, leopards and other animals hid in nooks and corners of the giant trees. Sometimes Silver Sparks sat on a branch and refused to fly forward. Iora kept whistling to get her going.

The rain had not relented even a little by the next night. Hungry and tired, they stopped on a large, flat branch, which was large enough to house a big Twitterland cottage. A garden of airplants grew on it, under the benevolent shade of the canopy. They had not managed to reach even the foot of the mountains by now in spite of all their effort. Beetle plucked some large leaves and built a tent to shelter the three of them together from the rainy night.

"Pray to the Angels that those Smudgestopper flowers have worked their magic on Beetle," said Owlus with a contorted nose.

Owlus and Iora only managed to get some edible red sponge leaves, which were far from delicious. Seeing them eat half-heartedly, Beetle went around in the dim light and rain, feeling with his hands. Finally, he got the Shakeberry Liana. He formed two leaf cups and slit one of the vines to get an orange berry-coloured liquid, which resembled a berry milk shake. Iora and Owlus were delighted to drink it and slept like rocks.

Beetle had just lied down when an owl began to hoot loudly. Due to the rain all the other night animals were quiet, but this one persisted pointlessly. Though Iora and Owlus slept soundly, Beetle couldn't sleep. He went out and requested the owl, who rolled its big eyes at him, to go to some other branch.

"This is my branch . . . You move your nest from here!" said the owl grouchily.

Beetle twisted and turned till the early morning hours when the owl finally retreated.

Rain came down with less intensity the next morning. Iora was fresh and ready to go. Owlus was finicky in the damp weather but he couldn't let anyone think that he was any less than Iora. Beetle was sleepy and sore but he pulled himself up. They proceeded after getting directions from Silver Sparks. Although the downpour had decreased, the dampness was quite trying.

"Who do you think can be the Twitter who joined hands with the anti-natural forces?" Iora asked Owlus.

This puzzle had been tormenting her mind but Beetle hadn't been able to give her satisfactory answers. She was glad she had a Twitter to discuss this with, even if it was Owlus.

With a superior look, Owlus replied, "Well . . . try to think who is the most suspicious-looking and meanest in Twitterland."

"If it hadn't happened seventy years back, I would think it was you," replied Iora.

Owlus opened his mouth to speak, but Iora started again, "The most untrustworthy I think would be Toucan. But he's quite young. It could be his father Toco Toucan."

"But their names do not start with 'Cooo', which the Ghost of Yellow Leaves said before he died. Caucal and Cuckoo are too young . . . Hmm . . . don't mind my saying this, but your grandfather is not exactly loved in Twitterland and his name does start with 'Cooo'."

"I shouldn't have asked for your twisted opinion!" Iora said as her brows came together in an unforgiving frown.

Cockatoo, after all, was her grandfather.

"Okay! All right! Don't fume like that. I said what I feel. Everyone is entitled to a free opinion," said Owlus.

Though Iora glared at Owlus, she kept thinking about his observation most unwillingly.

Finally, by noon, they entered the mountainous area. But just then the rain came back in a torrent, even worse than the day before. The strong winds accompanying the rain almost pushed them off the trees.

"What is that thing there on the ground?" shouted Iora above the din.

"Where?" asked Owlus.

"Right there, below," she pointed.

"Seems like a small cave," said Beetle, straining his eyes. "It is a cave! Let's climb down and go inside it for a while."

They climbed down the tree carefully. There was a gush of water on the mountain slope. They held hands and moved towards the cave on the steep, slippery ground.

It was a cosy little rock cave, well protected from the rain. They sat down dripping. Beetle took out some water-resistant sticks and his stones to light a fire. The insides of the cave lighted up. The small cave had a rocky end. The three sat down, drying their drenched clothes.

"What do you think would that be?" said Owlus, staring at the dead end of the cave. The flames had lighted up a carving on the wall. Owlus went for a closer look. To his surprise, there was an arrow carved on it aiming at a bow carved a little away. The bow was painted in red but the arrow was not. Iora reached out and touched the outline of the red bow. She got a feeling that the bow had started to move.

"Is this bow moving?" she asked.

"No, it's not," said Beetle, looking closely, "but its red paint is melting."

"Yes, it is," said Owlus, "and it is not just melting away, it is trickling through these cracks and climbing up towards the arrow!"

They watched in silence as the red colour went through a well-defined path towards the arrow and started filling it. When the arrow was red, the ground shook mildly. There appeared a crack in the rock between the bow and the arrow. The crack widened and a narrow path opened before them. Light filtered from the other end. They looked at each other and without speaking, Iora entered the gaping crack. Beetle and Owlus followed. In a flash, the crack closed behind them.

12
In the Amazing Land

They were stunned to see such incredible beauty. Blue rivers surged across the landscape; some had fascinating, vine-clad wooden bridges going across their swelling bellies. Choicest of trees and flowers, streams of various hues, orchids and blossoms making a riot of colours, velvety grass spreading beneath trees laden with sparkling fruits, paradise birds with long tails and spectacular plumages formed the scenery.

High above them, a thin, transparent membrane formed an umbrella covering the entire hinterland. They could see raindrops fall on it and slide sideways. The torrential sky was visible clearly through the membrane. There was an opening in it from where water fell on some crop fields. But what stood out in this backdrop were well-built and extraordinarily beautiful maidens.

These women, adorned with ivory armlets and

waistbands, had long, thick, curly hair and wore clothes woven out of plant fibres. Little girls played with miniature wooden bows, arrows and knives. An elephant, with tusks touching the ground, stood under a tree giving instructions to a group of young girls. Some older girls were gathered near a stream around a crocodile and jumped in the water one by one on its command. But there was something that was out of place with the beauty here. It was an elephant-sized rat that was half underground, digging trenches with its two teeth picks. An old woman instructed it where to dig.

"Wow! Is this an Angel's residence?" asked Owlus.

Before Iora could reply she felt something steely and cold touch her neck.

"Looks can be deceptive," came a voice.

The three of them cautiously turned around to see a tall, good-looking maiden clad in leather, pointing a knife at them – a knife with jagged teeth! Some more weapons were tucked in her clothes.

"Amazon!" exclaimed Beetle, looking thunderstruck.

"That's right. If you know us, you should have thought better than to come here!" she said in a steely voice.

"But it was accidental . . ." started Iora.

The Amazon pressed the knife on her neck. "No more talking! Come along."

Owlus's face took on a most comical expression on coming face to face with an Amazon. Beetle and Iora exchanged a sideways glance and obeyed her. They crossed the bridge, which lay right ahead of them with the Amazon at their rear. They looked below the bridge, at the deep waters; Iora jumped back as what she had thought to be a rocky bed in the water, moved out to reveal a huge crocodile. The waters were teeming with these creatures. Some opened their mouths wide to reveal their uneven teeth. And if that wasn't enough, the poisonous sting rays passed down under every now and then.

The Amazons stopped to look at them. Some looked curiously and others ferociously. "Who are they, guard?" asked many in one voice, to which the guard just shrugged her shoulders and said, "Intruders." Even the elephant came forward to have a closer look, and the elephant-sized rat stopped digging.

"They must be spies," said an old Amazon, lying on a hammock of latticeworked lianas.

"I like the fat Agogwe. He'll come handy in *Answering Anaconda Attack* training," said a young girl.

They were led to a sprawling tree under which two middle-aged women, terribly agile and swift, were practising moves for a fight. They stopped, seeing the strangers.

"What on earth . . ." grunted the older of the two.

Many Amazons gathered around them.

"I found them sneaking in through the arrow's mouth," answered the leather-clad guard bowing to them.

"How could anyone other than an Amazon open that mouth?" murmured the older woman to herself.

"Please let me explain? It was not intentional–" started Iora, when the older woman cut her short.

"Look here, girl, we do not know who you are and for what you came. The fact is that you are inside and no one sees Amazonland and leaves just like that. You must remain here now."

The trio stood shocked.

"But please if you may listen, I have been trading with Amazons for more than ten years," said Beetle desperately, "I barter with one tall lady with long, curly hair and black eyes." He looked around to realise that they all had long, curly hair and black eyes.

"Agogwe, you may have bartered with some of us, but that would be in the jungle, not in our homeland. We are warriors and we can't let any creatures, except the most trusted, know where we live."

"But please at least listen to us . . ." pleaded Iora.

"Our queen is not here. She will return only after two days. You can try pleading your case in front of her. I can't do anything, so no use wasting your breath on me," replied the woman.

"But we don't have two days to waste!" shouted Owlus.

"For all you know, young man, you may not be getting out of here for twenty more years. So don't worry about time," said the woman gesturing to the guard to take them away.

Two more guards, armed with knives and arrows, escorted them to a remote rock, on which were engraved an axe and a dagger. The dagger was painted black and the axe was not painted. One of the women placed her hand on the engraved dagger, and like the Bow and Arrow at the entrance, the black paint melted and flowed in the crevices towards the axe, colouring it black. Cracks appeared on the rock and it split open.

There was a small chamber inside with torches lit on its walls. Though their camouflage bags were not clearly visible, one of the Amazons reached out exactly to where they dangled from Owlus's and Iora's shoulders. They also took away Beetle's fibre bag and reached out and caught Silversparks hovering above Iora's head.

Iora cast one last look at the torrential sky through the membrane before they were pushed inside.

"Are you both okay?" asked Beetle once the rock closed.

"I am beside myself with joy!" answered Owlus.

"Was I dreaming or did you tell me once that you know how to deal with Amazons?" Iora asked Beetle crossly.

"Yes, I know how to barter with them but I am clueless about all this!"

"Thanks to both of you, I'll be scrubbing Amazons' plates for the rest of my life," babbled Owlus, looking pale.

"We've got to find a way out of this. And quickly!" said Iora.

"You know I've never seen them like this, I mean so adorned with flowers and all that. I've always seen them in rugged leather," said Beetle

"Don't worry, you'll get to see these flowery dresses a lot more," pointed Owlus.

Beetle shrugged himself out of the disbelief and said, "You see I've heard, and now I know for sure, that no one knows where Amazons live. They appear in the jungle and disappear at will. They're highly skilled warriors and are hired by many tribes who've to settle their differences with other tribes by way of war. But once you hire them they are in charge of the fight as well as the ones who've hired them. No one is ever known of losing a fight if they have Amazons on their side."

"Good detailing. It just made my hair stand straighter," said Owlus.

"They don't even bring their husbands or sons to Amazonland. Only their daughters are brought in," said Beetle.

"So that's that. Now how to get out?" said Iora, examining the chamber.

Five torches burned brightly, lighting up the place. In one corner there were some tightly shut containers made of animal bones. Iora lifted one of the lids to see roast meat in it. Another one had stir-fried headless bodies of honey ants which were considered a delicacy. The other pots were filled with juices, fruits, nuts and sweets. A giant empty eggshell of Elephant Bird was filled with fresh water. Three beds made of a giant insect's cocoons were placed in a corner with ratel skin blankets.

"This food is enough to last for a week at least. They are in no mood to get us out," sighed Beetle.

"This can't be! A week! We must get out of here tonight. One day has already gone down the drain," fumed Iora. "What will happen to Silversparks? What will they do to her?" she kept saying again and again.

"The question should be, *how* will we go ahead without her, if we ever escape?" Owlus corrected her.

They searched and searched but found no opening except another small chamber to be used as a bathroom. Exhausted and famished, they finally sat down to eat and gorged on the delicious food. Though they were in captivity, after many nights they had a good night's sleep in a cosy chamber.

The next day they got up late but didn't really know what time it was. Neither sun nor stars were visible to know the time. Iora was the most unsettled of the lot. They fretted and searched again.

"This can be opened only from the outside. There is no other way," said Beetle disheartened.

By what they thought was the end of the day, Iora and Owlus had already broken into fights twice, giving Beetle a tough time.

"They would let go two harmless kids but our chances were foiled due to His Highness Beetle Agogwe," Owlus would say.

"You . . . harmless indeed!" Iora would reply.

Finally, they drifted off to sleep.

Around midnight, there was a slight tremor and a muffled sound of rock rubbing against rock. Iora was the first to get up and wake the other two. They sat still, awaiting the unexpected. The rock opened and the dark cloudy night sent its humid air in, touching their faces and making the torch flames flicker. The three of them looked at a flame curving and bending with the breeze, throwing light on a familiar figure.

13
The Mountainous Forest

"Hoatzin! What on earth are you doing here?" exclaimed Iora. Owlus looked as if he'd not been happier to see anyone in his life before. Iora ran and hugged her as Hoatzin gestured Owlus and Beetle to get out of the cave. Silversparks came flying in a zigzag way, sat on Iora's hand and whistled a happy note.

"I'll answer all your questions later," said Hoatzin leading the way with an earthen lamp in her hand.

She led them on a different path. They crossed a couple of streams, a vineyard and a garden. Hanging baskets of night-glow orchids hung on the trees. There were holes in the tree trunks, some near the ground, others higher above. Amazons slept in them and small flames glittered inside each hole. They passed quietly. It was cloudy and some stars twinkled hazily in the distant sky. There was no membrane above Amazonland now.

Some crocodiles spotted them. Even a tree opened its beady eyes but went back to sleep. Owlus and Iora looked at each other with terror. But to their surprise, and relief, no one raised alarm. After a long walk they reached a steep rock. There was a large sword and its case engraved on it. The case was painted in purple. Hoatzin reached out and touched the case. The colour of the case melted and went through cracks towards the arrow, colouring it purple. The rock split open slowly, bringing forth the damp forest and the dark night beyond.

"You can proceed from here. It is a shorter way to reach the Insect Angel," said Hoatzin.

"But how do *you* know we're going after the Insect Angel?" asked Owlus.

"I said, Owlus, no questions right now," said Hoatzin in a calm voice.

"But won't you come along with us, Hoatzin?" asked Iora hopefully.

"No, little one, I am too old to join you," she replied, "and you don't have much time. I will meet you in Twitterland. May Nature be with you," she said, taking a few steps back. The rock closed in front of Hoatzin, leaving the trio at the mercy of the unknown wilderness.

***

"We must get out of the vicinity as soon as possible. There is still around three-quarters of the night remaining," said Beetle, looking at the stars.

They stood in a valley, encased in the dark silhouette of massive mountains cramped with tall vegetation. The multiple crooked hands of the trees stood like frozen ghosts against the dimly lit sky. The hanging vines made tattered curtains screening the starlight. They stood looking around until some night insects began their deafening racket nearby.

"Let's go," said Beetle to Iora and Owlus, who looked nervous at the enormity of the world about them.

They consulted Silversparks who flew in curves displaying the way ahead. The sparkling silver lines looked unnaturally bright on the dark background. They entered the forbidding mountainous jungle. Even the fireflies flew away from them. Voices from unseen forms tore through the night.

"Remember, the spirit of the jungle can be anywhere, in any form. We've to keep our eyes, ears and hearts open," murmured Iora.

"My heart and all other organs can only think of getting far away from our pretty armed ladies," said Owlus.

Iora and Owlus had no clue of mountainous forests and terrains. Beetle had only treaded in smaller hills but he'd never seen such huge forested mountains before. Owlus was thoroughly intimidated; he was actually mumbling disjointed rhymes and poems to relieve his fear. Iora looked at him with ridicule.

"What? I'm just practicing for my next Moonless-night performance!"

A blood-curdling scream rose from just a few paces away and echoed in the whole valley. A muffled sound accompanied a grunt and then everything fell silent.

"What was that?" asked Owlus, involuntarily holding Beetle's arm.

"Some creature has just been killed," answered Beetle.

"Wouldn't it be better if we walk on the trees and aerial highways?" suggested Iora, still staring in the direction from which the scream had originated.

"Wouldn't be any safer. Anyway, let's take the branch paths," said Beetle climbing one of the trees.

The first rays of the sun kissed the tree-tops, when the trio stopped to relax. The dark silhouettes had vanished bringing forth the actual forms. They had climbed to the top of the canopy to have an uninterrupted view of the landscape. The canopy was a green ocean of frozen waves; the sunrays shimmered on leaves, sending back glaring reflections. They were halfway to the mountain summit, and the valley from where they'd climbed was far below. Thick tree-tops covered the surrounding hilly giants. Intertwining tangles of vegetation seemed virtually indestructible. Insects of different sizes and shapes buzzing in the morning breeze looked like winged jewels.

But it didn't interest them much as their stomachs growled and they climbed down to freshen-up and eat something. After resting for a while Beetle said,

"Hoatzin was right. That was a shortcut. We'll reach our destination before dusk."

"I'll reach my destination when I'm back home," said Owlus lazily.

"All said and done, we've still wasted two days because of the rains and the Amazons' hospitality," said Iora, pulling a face.

By noon they were quite near the summit. When the sun cast a sideways glance, for they were on the other side of the mountain, Beetle consulted Silversparks for the way ahead. Silversparks blinked again and again instead of giving further directions.

"It should be somewhere here," Beetle said.

They looked around closely but could only see the thick jungle on all sides.

"Let's climb up a tree to get a better idea," suggested Owlus. They climbed up to the middle branches of a nearby tree, which had pointed leaves, but didn't see anything unusual. Silversparks blinked behind them.

"Shall we have some lunch before we proceed on our detective, prying endeavour?" asked Owlus looking at some small, bright red fruits hanging from a vine.

"How can you think of eating right now, Owlus?" said Iora in surprise.

"Don't even think of eating those fruits, Owlus. You would get a bloated stomach for days!" exclaimed Beetle. "These are rare Pincypin fruits and its paste with giant three-eyed squirrel fur is very effective to cure night limping disease. I could have traded this for a lot of goodies, but alas, it'll get spoilt by the time we get back." sighed Beetle.

"See, Iora, you wouldn't give your precious comments to Beetle who is daydreaming about his trade right now!"

They stood there as a faint buzzing sound echoed around, becoming louder and louder by the second.

"All I need right now is a giant bumblebee looking for food," Owlus mumbled.

But there was no insect in sight that could make such a sound. Silversparks had stopped fluttering and sat on Iora's shoulder. They had been standing in anticipation when they felt the tree move – or was it not the tree? It were the pointed leaves, which dispersed in thousands from the tree and floated in mid air.

14
The Insect Angel's Guide

On a closer look they realised that those were not leaves but leaf-shaped insects with tiny legs, pointed stings and small red eyes. Owlus was dazed looking at the sight of a thick cloud of buzzing insects pointing their stings at them. He moved backwards. Iora stood frozen. Beetle gaped and held his beard tightly. The swarm of insects closed in on them from all sides. Iora desperately looked around for a hole or a crevice in the tree but to no avail.

"Owlus . . . Hold on!" shouted Beetle.

But it was too late. Owlus slipped from the edge of the branch and fell down the soaring tree. His shriek was drowned in the buzzing sound that engulfed him. Beetle and Iora watched shocked and helpless, their hands on their heads, as a piece of the green cloud rushed after the falling form. Owlus plummeted down and was about to crash when Iora turned away with her hands covering her ears. But there was no thud, no shriek.

She slowly turned to see Owlus hanging in mid air, a whisker above the ground, the piece of green cloud holding him. Before they could speak, thousands of green insects came and held them all over their bodies with their tiny legs. Iora and Beetle found themselves floating in the air like Owlus. The insects took the three of them higher above. They didn't try to shake them off, as they knew if they did they would either die of thousands of stings or of falling down. Silversparks followed Iora close behind.

They were brought in front of a monster spider web, which was no less than five to six hundred feet tall, stretching from the top of the canopy to the bottom. Nothing could be seen beyond it. Some of the green insects went hovering near it and made a knuckle shape. The floating knuckle then knocked on the supple web a couple of times. Someone opened part of the web from the other side and the web started to dissolve, making a hole, large enough to take them in.

They went on the other side and found themselves above the canopy of the forest as the web closed behind them. They couldn't believe what they saw. Instead of the emerald expanse of the canopy, there was a crazy variety of flowers in a riot of colours, brilliantly painted butterflies and hummingbirds flitted amongst exotic blossoms, insects of all shapes and sizes hovered, darted and suspended themselves in the scented air – their humming and whining in the sea of flowers a restful chant. The strangeness and beauty of this scene quite surpassed the wondrous Amazonland. This beauty was somewhat eerie, displaying forms, shapes, colours and scents not just unique, but unbelievable. On the fringes of this divine panorama, the green of the usual jungle was visible and so were some distant mountains with silvery lines of waterfalls. The three of them hung in mid air when a five-footed, six-eyed spider emerged from a flowerbed. The leafy insects let go of their hold at the sight of the spider and the three landed on a velvety bunch of indigo flowers. The other insects didn't take any notice as the green cloud flew away to settle down on their post on the bare tree again.

The spider stood at a distance but four of its eyeballs fell on the plants and rolled towards the trio. The eyeballs circled them and after examining carefully went rolling back to the spider and up their respective sockets.

The spider said in a grating voice, "You are late."

Iora and Beetle stood up and Owlus fumbled to stand straight on the soft flower floor.

"Insect Angel, I can't tell you how honoured . . . how utterly privileged . . . I am to see you . . . to hear your voice . . . to be standing in front of you . . ." stammered Beetle at the sight of the Angel that his tribe worshipped.

"Beetle, I don't think this could be the Angel . . ." Iora whispered but he was too overwhelmed to reason.

"Please let me touch your sacred feet . . ." he continued, glancing down at the eight legs of the spider, wondering which one to touch first.

"I am *not* the Insect Angel!" rattled the spider.

"What . . . you're not?!" said Beetle.

"Foolish Agogwe, you think I am the divine Insect Angel who distributes the sunrays to the jungle with its sting! Where do you see my sting? And where do you think are the Angel's wings which control the cycles of the seasons? Anyway, the Angel awaits you. Come this way," clattered the spider.

Owlus chuckled at Beetle in spite of his dread of the spider.

They reached a giant crimson flower with fleshy petals growing amidst a bunch of long warped flowers.

"That must be Rafflesia, the largest flower on earth," whispered Iora.

"Good time to flaunt your 'knowledge', Iora," Owlus sneered.

Beetle, still flushed on mistaking the spider for the Angel, looked around in anticipation.

"You are standing in the presence of the Great Insect Angel," rattled the spider, all its six eyes fixed on the flower.

"But where is the Angel?" asked Iora.

"Can't you see, Twitter? I thought the Bird Angel worshippers had extraordinary sight," clattered the spider.

"Do you mean this *flower* is the Insect Angel?" inquired Owlus.

"It is me you're looking for," came a soothing voice, and they saw a tiny scorpion move on the crimson petals of the Rafflesia flower.

"You're mistaken, we're looking for the Insect Angel," said Beetle, trying not to repeat the blunder.

"Blind fellows! Who do you think is standing in front of you?" snarled the spider, staring at them with all its six eyes, which was enough to convince them.

Beetle got down on his knees in front of the tiny scorpion but didn't say anything. Though perplexed, Iora also bowed. She had heard the description of the Insect Angel from her father but that didn't have any mention of his size.

"Now I know where the Insect Angel followers get their height from . . ." Owlus giggled under his breath.

The scorpion turned on his tiny legs towards Owlus and he gaped at him. He seemed a bit larger than before. Before Owlus could voice his doubt, the Angel expanded and within moments he was three times the size of Owlus, Iora and Beetle put together. His black body with a sizzling razor sharp sting towered above them. The Rafflesia flower seemed a small poppy in front of it.

"Strength is not size dependent, and neither is substance," came the smooth voice, not amplified with the size.

Owlus had a strong urge to flee the site, forgetting he

had come looking for the Insect Angel. But he got down to his knees in wonder and terror.

"Where do you want me to come?" asked the large scorpion.

"On the bank of the Scar-faced River near Twitterland, Angel," replied Iora respectfully.

"Then I'll be there on the coming moonless night. But I must warn you . . ." said the scorpion stretching, to the trio's surprise, a pair of black wings that seemed to come out of his shell. He furled them and they seemed to disappear in his black shell again. But on looking intently, Iora realised that they had not disappeared, but stuck closely to the shell in a camouflage.

The Angel continued after a pause, "But I must warn you that the way forward is not going to be as easy as it has been so far."

"Did he say 'easy'?" Owlus whispered.

"The dark force knows now what you're up to. Its agents will be stalking you and will try to put an end to your mission. You don't have much time and there is a lot at stake," he said in his even voice, moving gently on the flowers without crushing them.

A thrilled Beetle gazed at the Angel in awe.

The Insect Angel's message was clear. They had to hurry up. More difficulties on the way meant they would be slowed down further.

"Your job is done here. May the Nature be with you," said the Angel.

The spider shifted to lead them away.

Silversparks sat on the silver sting of the Angel, seeming quite at home.

"Is Silversparks going to stay with you, Angel?" asked Owlus softly, his intimidated gaze fixed on the silver sting. He had realised Silversparks was in no mood to fly further.

"She has come back home and I don't think will undertake another journey just as yet," said the Angel, as Silversparks sat there closing and opening her wings slowly.

"Then can you give us the directions please?" asked Iora.

"Giving directions will not make any sense. Directions are given for a fixed destination, which I am afraid you don't have. However, there can't be a better help than Baba. Webster will lead you to him," the Insect Angel said, turning his head towards the spider.

Beetle was still on his knees. Iora had to shake him to get him going. They all thanked and paid their respects again to the Angel who had already shrunk and stepped onto the Rafflesia flower, which was his abode. Silversparks came fluttering towards Iora and whistled a goodbye note as Iora stroked her wings fondly one last time.

And so the company of three went down the splendid world of flowers and leaves, following Webster who sometimes tottered ahead of them and at others descended by a thick thread of saliva coming out of his hairy mouth. They crossed the monster web and went down the canopy. Owlus eyed the spider's eyes, suspecting them to roll towards him any moment.

"Baba is the best guide and protector that the Insect Angel could have granted. You should be thankful to your last bone. Though Baba is a little short of hearing and old, he is unmatched!" rattled Webster, hanging upside down.

"Short of hearing and old!" muttered Owlus under his breath.

Webster stopped on a large branch, somewhere near the lower end of the tree.

An old, over-overweight ape with a very kind face and a triple chin hanging down right to the bottom of his tummy sat munching on a branch. This was an orangutan with a large forehead and body covered with long, tousled foxy red hair.

"This is Baba," rattled Webster.

Baba looked at them and continued munching nonchalantly.

"You must be kidding me!" exclaimed Owlus, no longer able to communicate his feelings in a whisper.

"Baba, you know what the Insect Angel wants," continued Webster, speaking to Baba but looking sternly at Owlus.

"No, don't explain, Webster, I know what the Insect Angel wants," said Baba.

"This guy is deaf!" Owlus's comments had again gone down to a murmur looking at Webster's gaze.

"Shall we? We're pretty short of time," said Baba getting up with effort, the knuckles of his long hands placed firmly on the branch. He looked almost upright even though his hands were placed down. His rusty long hair made him look more haggard.

"Many thanks, Sir Webster," said Iora to the spider who had turned to go, his six distrusting eyes still fixed on Owlus.

They followed Baba who slowly lugged his heavy mass towards the trees in the front.

"We must hurry up," said Baba, moving rather unhurriedly himself.

Even Iora and Beetle, their awe at the Insect Angel having waned a little, exchanged a look of doubt.

They had hardly covered any distance when night fell. Jungle resounded with night voices.

"We're going very, very slowly!" shouted Iora to the hard hearing Baba who'd sat down to relax.

"Don't speak so loudly, you're scaring away the night animals! And well... progress towards the goal does not depend on the speed, but the path taken," Baba said and Iora frowned. "We should spend the night here and start early tomorrow," he continued. "I'll get food. Light up a fire, Beetle," he said, plucking some reddish-green leaves and laying them down on the branch.

"Over these leaves?" said Beetle, astonished.

"No, in the middle of them. These are Bor-bor Bonfire leaves," said Baba swinging away. He was soon out of sight in the all-encompassing darkness.

"Such a useful bit of information! I must make a note of the tree's name," said Beetle happily. "And Sir Baba is such a well-mannered, gentle animal" he concluded, glowing about the fact that someone had gone to get food for him for a change.

But Iora and Owlus hardly noticed the gesture.

"A well-mannered, gentle animal! I thought the guide was going to be some fluttering insect like Silversparks! I hope he returns before breakfast," fumed Owlus.

Iora didn't say anything. In spite of herself, she agreed with Owlus. She had become extremely restless with their slow pace. She tried to look at the moon to see how thin it had become and how far was the moonless night, but the sky was not visible from there.

She felt someone staring at her. Could be an owl, she thought and looked around absent-mindedly when she caught sight of two blood-red eyes fixed on her.

Startled, she asked, "Who is it?"

Owlus and Beetle also looked in the direction of the eyes, alerted.

The eyes slowly advanced towards Iora in the flickering light of the fire.

15
Homo-lamia and Post Chimps

A pale woman, with straight hair falling on her face, walked towards Iora on all fours. She smiled, exposing her jagged, pointed teeth. Torn shreds of animal skin draped her body and dark bones peeped out of her translucent skin. Iora was terrified and looked around for a place to run. She was in the middle of the branch and if she ran either ways, the woman could jump and catch her.

"Oh my pretty baby . . . don't be scared, we've met before," uttered the woman in a high-pitched voice, drawing near Iora.

"We've never met before!" shrieked Iora.

She leaped towards Iora just as Iora jumped down from the branch. Owlus and Beetle, who were on the far corner of the branch, ran towards her and saw that the woman had caught her with her bony hands. She then stuck out her tongue and poured a thick liquid out of her mouth, which spread on the branch.

"Don't you dare do anything to her!" shouted Beetle. Owlus had taken a log in his hand.

"He! He! He!" she cackled drawing her tongue inside and pulling Iora back to the branch.

Just then, they heard a rustling of leaves overhead and Baba came swinging down with his hands full. "What's going on?" he shouted. From his side, only Beetle and Owlus were in view.

Before he could land on the branch, the creature disappeared, leaving a shaken Iora behind. Owlus and Beetle rushed towards her. She came with them near the fire; her curly hair dangled on her flushed face.

"What happened here?" asked Baba.

"Now we'll be damaging our vocal cords explaining to him," scowled Owlus.

"A little damage to your vocal cords wouldn't hurt. We can do without you wise cracks," said Baba to everyone's surprise.

"But you can't hear properly . . ." said Owlus.

"I hear when I need to hear," Baba replied.

All three of them looked at Baba intrigued.

"It seems a *Homo-lamia* had come along, this place is reeking of her! But they are harmless," Baba said, his creased face showing no emotion.

"But that creature, *Homo-lamia* or whatever, nearly killed Iora!" exclaimed Beetle.

"Everything that looks ugly is not wicked. *Homo-lamia* and *Homo-malus* are scattered communities in the jungle; you call them half-human jungle witches and wizards. They live solitarily, and most of the time, in hiding. They undergo metamorphosis every month. They start as an aquatic animal, then transform into aquatic semi-human, then reptile, then human-reptile, then sub-human and finally human-witch or human-wizard each month. After the moonless night they start their metamorphosis all over again from the aquatic animal stage. They mostly eat insects and sometimes suck animal blood like the vampire bats."

"Harmless indeed! She could have sucked the blood out of us!" said Owlus.

"They do not suck to kill. Do you die of a mosquito bite?" asked Baba. "She had just come to gorge on insects which would have been lethal if they'd bitten Iora," he said, pointing at the sticky saliva of *Homo-lamia* which shone in the light of the fire and had a couple of bark-shaped insects trapped in it.

"She said we'd met before. Why did she say that?" asked a trembling Iora.

"She was wearing a hat? No, no, they don't wear hats!" said Baba, who seemed to have lost his sense of hearing.

"That horrible creature said she'd met Iora!" shouted Owlus in Baba's ears.

"So what can I say? Iora should know better," he said, and got busy cooking over fire.

"Why did she say that? Was she lying?" Iora asked Beetle and Owlus again and again without getting any satisfactory answers. Baba had spread all that he'd collected around him and sat in the middle.

"I don't know what kind of food we'll get. I better go and gather some things for myself," said Owlus.

Iora was too preoccupied to think of food.

"Sir Baba, may I help?" asked Beetle, approaching Baba.

"I don't like this Sir-ring business. Just call me Baba," replied Baba, who seemed to have regained his hearing power. "I'll be done shortly."

It was in no time that the usually slow Baba had prepared a variety of dishes and laid them out around the fire in leaf plates and mugs. "Food is ready," he said to the trio who sat on the farther end of the huge branch.

Even Iora forgot about what had conspired when she laid her eyes on the dinner – some of it cooked and not raw! There were roasted mushrooms, hot sweetened deer milk, a misty Fumefruit drink, a tropical fruit salad and a root and herb soup prepared on the fire proof leaf bowl.

"So what are you waiting for? Go on!" said Baba grumpily.

They ate the food with gusto, not pausing for even a breath. Beetle quickly made make-shift tents for the three of them after dinner and Baba laid down on the branch. Iora and Owlus slept soundly, their stomachs full and satisfied.

The next morning they started on their journey again. By this time they had stopped eyeing Baba with suspicion. His pace was better but he took uncanny routes – sometimes from within the hollow of a tree trunk, at others from secret mountain tunnels that came out at unexpected places. He was always in the lead and would suddenly stop them, especially Iora, from crossing a puddle of water or touching a branch, as if he had eyes concealed at the back of his shaggy head. They travelled like this for two days.

***

In which direction are we headed? We've been changing direction so frequently, wondered Beetle.

"All destinations are not reached by following one direction," replied Baba, without looking back.

"Now . . . you do know what you're doing, old ape?" asked Owlus, who was now much more protected and well-fed in Baba's company.

Baba didn't answer. Beetle had felt his burden of responsibility become considerably lighter in the past two days. He was looked after and felt stress-free. Iora was resigned to the proceedings. She was quiet but her mind was a cacophony of thoughts – was her grandpa Cockatoo involved in any way, why did *Homo-lamia* look strangely familiar, would they reach Twitterland with all the Angels on the moonless night, what if they didn't find the Spirit of the Jungle, how had she opened the Amanzonland doorway when she was a Twitter, what was Hoatzin doing in Amazonland, was her father safe . . .

"Today, around afternoon, we may cross the fringes of the regular forest before entering the Wacky Wilderness again," informed Baba.

"Now that's good news," said Iora. "We can catch hold of a Post Chimp to send a message home!"

"So can I," chirped Owlus. "Mother and father would have gone nuts by now. And Fowlus will feel better knowing her bright brother is fine."

"Father wouldn't have returned . . . Don't know how Grandpa would be . . ." sighed Iora.

"I won't advise you to send a message. But you may if you wish to," said Baba in his deep yet expressionless voice.

"Why?" asked Owlus and Iora simultaneously, but their question went unheard.

By afternoon they had entered the regular forest. For an untrained eye, there was no difference. The regular forest appeared the same as the Wacky Wilderness. For a non-jungle dweller, even the regular forest would look quite wacky.

"I had asked Bara, my *Homo-avis* friend, to communicate my message to my family. They wouldn't be worried," said Beetle. "A little message of safety wouldn't hurt, but my problem is dealing with the Post Chimps."

"Pot-belly, I'll show you how to do it," said Owlus.

"Can't we send Owlus also along with the message?" asked Iora.

Iora hoped fervently to come across a Post Chimp, though she'd never sent messages before. They couldn't have walked a long distance but before much time had elapsed, they came across a troupe of chimpanzees playing and swinging on branches. Iora and Owlus beamed at the sight of those chimpanzees.

"If you are sending a message, neither give your whereabouts nor mention where you're headed," suggested Baba.

"But do we even know where we're headed?" asked Owlus advancing towards the troupe.

The chimpanzees stopped playing and began to laugh at Owlus.

"What's so funny, primates?" asked Owlus, who stopped nibbling on the muncher-puncher nut.

"A little rose powder on your cheek and you are ready!" said one of them, and they all giggled again.

Owlus touched his head and found a string of flowers tied to his hair. He took it out and threw it away. A little chimp scurried away from behind.

Baba had climbed a branch to look for insects. Just then a baby chimp came along and snatched away the muncher-puncher nut from Owlus's hand.

"These jokers should be fed to the Head Hunters!" said Owlus. He turned away and fell down flat on his face. A chimp had tied the straps of his monitor lizard skin shoes. The chimpanzees looked extremely pleased; they jumped on their feet and showed their teeth and gums.

"Okay, that's enough!" said Beetle coming forward. "We want to send a message to Twitterland."

A young chimpanzee came forward. "Tell me," he said mischievously, "I am a Post Chimp."

"You give your message before they start their pranks again," whispered Beetle to Iora.

"Include that I'm also with you," said Owlus, no longer in the mood to send a message.

"This is for my grandpa Cockatoo in Twitterland," began Iora, "Beetle, Owlus and I are safe and sound and halfway through our mission. Don't worry, I'll be home before the moonless night," she said, and then requested, "Can you please repeat the message for me?"

The chimp cheerfully started to recite the message:

"Cockatoo Grandpopsie on the moonless night,
Do I have to be home? Um . . . all right . . .
Beetle will bring the safe; Owlus will make the sound,
The mission halfway, well . . . we'll soon be found."

"What kind of nonsense is this?" Iora said impatiently; Owlus looked contented that he'd not given a message. Beetle nudged Iora with his elbow.

She hesitated and then said, "Uh . . . I didn't communicate the message clearly it seems. I'll say it again . . . um . . . okay here goes:

Beetle, Owlus and I are fine
Our mission is going all right
Don't worry, we're safe and sound
Will be back before the moonless night
If this kind Post Chimp delivers my note
Feel a little stress-free – you might"

The chimps were happy to hear this. The Post Chimp repeated the message correctly this time. Some of the chimps came tittering towards them and the little ones held their hands, inviting them to play. Owlus was revolted by the idea.

Baba's grumpy voice came from the branches, "Are we done yet?"

Bidding farewell to the chimps and walking for some time, they stopped near a stream to relax for a while. Beetle went to relieve himself, as his stomach had not fully recovered. Owlus and Iora sat down near the stream, gathered some Foul Mouthed seeds, which screamed filthy words when plucked, and started playing Shut the Squeak. They noticed three lavender-coloured fruits hanging precariously from a vine on a high branch. They emitted a misty mauve light.

"Wow, those must be Paradise Fruits!" said Owlus, his jaw dropping, as he chucked his silky hair off his eyes.

"Yes . . . so they are," said Iora. "Father had told me they taste heavenly, but they have to be eaten immediately after plucking so he can't bring them from the forest."

"How delicious they look," said Owlus.

"But I've heard it is very difficult to pluck them. They start crying star-shaped tears, which are acidic."

"The climb is very difficult . . ." mumbled Owlus, undecided but tempted.

"Leave it then. Don't land yourself in any kind of trouble at this time. I do not want to get late if you break a leg," warned Iora.

Owlus thought for a while and then looked at Baba who sat looking for insects on the ground with a twig.

"Baba, old buddy, I've never ever tasted that in my life. Can you pleeeeease bring down just one tiny-winy Paradise Fruit?" pleaded Owlus.

It seemed the request had gone unheard.

After looking for insects for a couple of minutes, Baba glanced at Owlus.

"This is a time wasting exercise in the middle of the day. But since there is no sign of Beetle, I'll get some for both of you."

Baba got up, his long, rusty hair hanging from his bulky body. He had climbed up the tree and was lost in the thick foliage, when Beetle arrived.

"Oh, what relief!" he said, rubbing his stomach. "Where is Baba?"

"He has just gone up to get us Paradise Fruits," informed Iora.

"Are you serious?!" he said brightening up, and sat down to wait.

Unusually melodious croaking notes came floating in the wind.

"What kind of sound is that?" Iora asked Beetle.

"Never heard the likes of it before," he answered, puzzled but enjoying the toe tapping music.

They followed the sound and spotted a small frog seated on a lily leaf. The brilliant cherry and yellow skin was its most striking feature. They went near the edge of the stream to have a closer look. Owlus slipped on the algae and held Iora's long hair to stop from falling.

"Are you going to leave my hair or what!" she shouted.

The frog stopped croaking and looked scared.

"You have some talent there, little fellow," said Beetle.

The frog asked in a croaky yet sweet voice, "Are you all Twitters?"

"Does this shorty looks like a Twitter to you?" Owlus was shocked.

The frog said in a sweet, sad voice, "It seems I am the only one left of my kind . . . Every day I live in fear of extinction. My kind was only confined to this stream and we didn't have any predators. But recently the snakes have grown in abundance and they come out at night to hunt. It is difficult for me to hide; I have such bright colours. Every day for me is a bonus and so I sing my heart out, hoping someone will hear me and take me to safety, even as a pet . . ."

"Why pet, we can just rescue–" Iora began when Owlus cut her short.

"Yes, you can be my pet. I spotted you and I'm your saviour, right?"

Owlus was all excited at the thought of showing off a singing frog in Twitterland. "Come here, I'll take you along." Owlus sat on the ground and reached towards the lily leaf.

The frog shrank from Owlus's outstretched hands. "Are you really nice people?" it asked fearfully.

"Yes, yes, bonehead. We're *very* nice people. Now hop onto my hand!" said Owlus.

But the frog retreated further.

Owlus stood up, frustrated, and turned to Beetle. "Can you catch it for me?"

Beetle was not too keen on catching the frog, but he was not used to refusing children. So he bent down and reached out. Iora watched interestedly.

She didn't stop Beetle, as she really wanted to rescue the frog. And she trusted Beetle to make the frog feel less anxious.

Beetle caught the edge of the lily leaf, slowly pulled it towards him and held the frog gently in his hand. "It is okay, little fellow," he said kindly.

"I said NO!" croaked the frog, its voice more raucous than before.

Before Beetle could say something, Baba's heavy voice came from above, "Leave it at once!"

Baba climbed down the trunk hurriedly and let go of the sparkling Paradise Fruits, which fell down on the ground with a splash. In a fraction of a second the frog opened its mouth wide. They could see a forked white tongue and two sharp red fangs on either side. It slithered out of Beetle's hand and hopped onto his neck inserting its red fangs deep into it. Beetle's breathing stopped and his eyes rolled. The frog disappeared in the stream before Iora or Owlus could understand what was going on. Beetle fell, face down in the stream, looking unconscious, or rather . . . dead.

16
The Dark Forces Strike

Beetle floated face down in the stream. Owlus was frozen, fear clutching his heart, and Iora stood with her hands on her mouth, unable to utter a word. Baba hurried towards the stream and pulled Beetle out of the water.

"Is he . . . dead?" stammered Owlus.

Baba observed the wound where the frog had bitten. Beetle's whole face had turned a greenish pink.

"Please do something!" Iora finally said, her fists clenched and eyes full of tears.

Baba left Beetle and climbed a tree with startling agility. He came down in a moment with a honey-filled leaf cup. Scarlet bubbles constantly rimmed and burst in the cup. He quickly applied it on the wound.

"Let's hope she's nearby," he whispered, and then made a sharp piercing noise, standing at the edge of the water.

He looked up and down the stream. Nothing happened. He made the same sound again. Still nothing happened. Baba's straight face now showed concern. He went a little inside the stream and was about to call again when an elongated form rose out of the water near him. It was a gigantic eel standing upright, face to face with Baba, its lower end submerged in water.

"Good to see you after fifty years, Baba, or has it been more?" she said in the same sharp voice in which Baba had made the calls.

Her long body had a pattern of dull yellow crisscross lines and two black eye slits stared out of her head, which was covered with red hair.

"Yes, yes, Healer Eelu, it has been long. We have an emergency," said Baba, pointing towards Beetle whose whole body had now turned a rather worrisome green.

"Bring him to me," said Eelu, her eyes narrowing on Beetle.

Baba lifted him and brought him near her. Beetle's wheezing breaths came sporadically, shaking him each time.

"This can't be . . . have they again . . . these children . . ." she said shocked.

"Yes, that's right. Please help us," implored Baba.

"When I heard you some streams down, I had no idea!" said the Healer, examining the two pointed marks with her snout.

Iora shook away her initial shock and came towards

them. "Please tell me nothing is going to happen to Beetle . . ."

The eel looked at her, her eyes not looking so scary now. "Don't worry, child. May Nature be with us."

Glancing down the stream to where Baba held Beetle in his hands, Iora saw that there was no end to the eel's body. It stretched upstream till her eyes could see. Healer Eelu touched some adjoining weeds in the stream and they all grew in length. These weeds entangled with each other in a bed shape suspended above the stream. Baba placed Beetle on it. The giant eel threw out a thick auburn liquid from her mouth into the water. It didn't sink, dissolve or flow away but kept floating near her. She opened her mouth and Iora and Owlus saw some of her jagged teeth take the shape of surgery tools.

When they were of the right size, she let them fall near Beetle on the suspended bed. She arranged five to six teeth apparatus on the bed with her snout and spat some seeds on the bank. Within moments, bushes with cotton flowers had sprouted around. Baba stood on alert, waiting to help.

Healer Eelu soon commenced the surgery, picking the tools one by one in her mouth. She stopped halfway and looked around for something. Spotting it on the other side of the stream, she swam and returned with a fleshy flower in her mouth. She lowered it down to where the frog had bitten. The flower widened its base, revealing pointed suckers and closed itself hungrily on Beetle's throat.

"What's going on?" asked Iora with apprehension.

"Getting rid of bad blood," answered Baba.

Once the flower was done, the eel applied the thick orange floating liquid, placed cotton on it and tied it with medicinal weeds around the neck. Baba opened Beetle's mouth and the eel put a few drops of a clear pink liquid in it.

"This will banish pain but may induce complete or partial forgetfulness for a few days," informed Healer Eelu.

The bed was then lowered to the dry bank as Eelu blew air from her nostrils on the weeds. Iora and Owlus approached Beetle, both looking extremely anxious.

"Just open his eyes," said Eelu.

Baba opened one of Beetle's eyes. Frightened shrieks escaped from Iora and Owlus. Beetle's eyes had turned dark green and the black pupil was hardly visible.

"I've done my best, Baba. Let's hope the poison recedes," said the eel. "If his eyes start resuming normal colour by daybreak tomorrow, he'll be fine. But he needs complete rest – now as well as for days following his recovery. What will you do?" she asked with concern.

Baba was lost in thought for a while. "I know where his clan would be housing this time of the year. Thank Angels it is not far from here. They don't stay at one place for more than six to seven days. We'll be able to catch up with them, if what I remember is correct," he answered.

"But how long will it take? It is only thirteen days to the moonless night," said Healer Eelu.

Iora and Owlus looked at each other, wondering how the Healer Eelu knew about it.

"We'd lose one day at most if we take the detour," said Baba, "and we should get going immediately."

"Should we all lift him up?" asked Iora.

"That wouldn't be necessary. I'll call the spiders to make a web swing to carry him," said Baba.

"No, he needs to go very comfortably. I'll arrange a stretcher," said Healer Eelu moving to the other side of the stream, part of her body still erect above water.

She hissed facing the jungle on the other side. A row of walking fur came towards her. She put down her snout on the other bank. A part of her elongated body came above water and touched the other side of the bank, connecting both the sides of the stream.

The fur line climbed on her snout and crossed the stream on her body. When the line descended on their end Iora realised that they were large millipedes with fur-covered backs. The millipedes got together in a rectangular block, inches above the ground, and Baba placed Beetle on to it. Healer Eelu again stood erect in water.

"I think you know their tongue, Baba. They don't understand Jungly," she said.

Baba nodded. “Let’s hope we meet before another fifty years have passed.”

“Yes, hopefully. Let’s hope everything is well with the jungle when we meet next. And yes, keep checking the Agogwe’s eyes. May the Nature be with you . . .”

The fur stretcher took Beetle forward and Owlus and Baba turned to go. But Iora stood there looking at Healer Eelu.

“What is it, little Twitter?” asked the Healer.

Baba and Owlus turned towards them.

“I have a feeling . . . can you be the . . . Spirit of the Jungle?” asked Iora.

The eel smiled. “Good observation I must say. Yes, I was the Spirit of the Jungle once. But the Spirit changes every few years. I do hope you find it,” she answered, slowly going deep into the water.

Iora stood looking after her as she disappeared in the stream.

By nightfall they’d reached the Scar-faced River, which flowed down to Twitterland. They had not entered the Wacky Wilderness again as they had to leave Beetle to safety with his folks. Owlus felt very guilty.

He kept mumbling, “If only I’d not asked Beetle to get the frog . . .”

Guilt gnawed on him each time he saw the green-tinged Beetle on the fur-stretcher rolling on the ground. Iora was quiet but she too felt guilty. The feeling of concern was much more pronounced in her than guilt.

Beetle had been her best friend cum mentor. "Nothing can happen to him!" she kept telling herself.

Baba checked Beetle's eyes a number of times but they were still a ghastly green. They finally stopped near the Scar-faced River's bank.

"We'll spend the night here," informed Baba, and lit a small fire a little distance away.

The stretcher also sat on the ground. Baba didn't want to leave them alone so he climbed up the adjoining trees and got fruits and nuts. But neither of the children touched the food.

Drawing a sigh he began, "Be clear that it is not your fault. The dark anti-natural forces are becoming stronger. Sympathy-Singer Frog is their tool and had come for Iora, to put an end to this mission. But incidentally, Beetle reached out and not her."

Iora and Owlus looked stunned.

"This can't be!" said Iora

"This is the truth. Both of you should be extra careful. One cannot live without trusting others. But be mindful of whom you trust," said Baba.

"But what about Beetle, will he be all right?" asked Owlus.

"Some answers only time can give," said Baba. "Patience is not called a virtue for no reason. You both have to be strong if you want to achieve your goal and confront the dark forces. So better eat something."

Beetle shook with each breath. They both ate a little

and went to sleep with a heavy heart, after checking Beetle's eyes, which were still dark green in colour.

17
Farewell to Beetle

Iora lay awake for long, lost in thoughts and unable to sleep. After getting up and looking at Beetle a number of times, she finally drifted off to sleep. They woke up at the crack of dawn and the first thing they did was approach Beetle and check his eyes. At long last! They breathed a sigh of relief; his eyes were a lighter green now and his breathing was less erratic, almost regular.

The day was very bright here as the forest canopy did not cover the river and the sun reflected vividly on the waters. Beetle's improving condition and the brilliant sun brightened up their spirits. They ate their breakfast with Baba smiling down at them. The fur stretcher was also up on its multitude feet, ready to go.

"We have to cross the river," Baba said to the fur millipedes in their language.

The fur stretcher turned at a right angle to see Baba.

"I know you can't cross waters. Do not worry, I'll arrange for something."

Iora and Owlus looked at the wide ruddy rainforest river flowing gently, its depth imperceptible.

"How are we going to cross it? We do not have a canoe," said Iora.

"This is the same river that flows near Twitterland. Back home we have very good vessels to cross it. And then you have all sorts of unwanted crocodiles and anacondas in it," added Owlus. The back of a huge yellow and green reptile could be seen slithering near the bank.

"I will call the hippos to take us to the other end by forming a float," said Baba, climbing a tree to gain a broader view.

"Hippo Float indeed!" said Owlus, who had been regaining his spirits with Beetle's recovering health. "These hippos turn the floats of so many Twitters. We're going to ride a float of the float turners! Excellent idea I must say!"

Baba came back in a while and said, "There are not enough hippos to carry all of us."

Owlus uttered a brief 'Thank Angels'.

"But thankfully, Pink River Dolphins are there. I would have preferred Hippo Float Formation as it is more stable, but dolphins should serve our purpose. I've called six hippos to take Beetle's bed and we can cross on dolphins' backs," said Baba, picking up a few flat pink stones from the bank.

He tossed them vertically and they bounced on the water five to six times, emitting musical notes with each bounce. He stopped but the musical notes echoed and grew louder.

A pink smiling face of a dolphin came out of water. Baba patted him on the head amiably.

"Sir Baba, we stand at your command," said the dolphin pleasantly.

"Not again. No Sir-ring with me and no 'command' talk too," said Baba, quite awkward at the formal address.

"But if we're not going to Sir the Great Baba, who are we going to!" exclaimed the dolphin.

"Anyway, we need your help. The four of us need to cross the river. We have a very sick Agogwe and he has to be taken to the other end. Hippos will be taking him. Can you take the rest of us?"

The dolphin turned around in circles and said in a musical voice, "What an honour to be of help to you, Sir. I'll call the others right away!"

He went splashing ahead, his pink form shining in the sunrays against the ruddy backdrop.

Meanwhile the hippos arrived. One of them came on land and bowed to Baba. Baba bowed back. The hippo staggered with surprise and bowed even further down.

"How well I can do without all this," Baba sighed.

"Sir Baba, we are here at your service. I regret that other hippos are not around," said the hippo.

"Oh no, it is okay. We didn't need more of you. The Pink Dolphins will help us," said Baba.

The hippo went inside the river and all the six of them came together, their rounded backs levelled against each other forming a float in the water. The fur millipedes happily marched on the hippos' backs with their heads held high, feeling superior to the giant hippos at their service.

A happy bunch of dolphins arrived and their musical greetings created a racket.

"This Baba guy seems to be a celebrity here," muttered Owlus.

The group of Pink Dolphins fought over carrying Baba while the hippos started floating with Beetle. Iora looked anxiously at the stretcher.

Soon the three of them were sitting on three dolphins – their legs dangling in water and hands holding the fins. The dolphin carrying Baba was so excited that she leapt again and again in the air merrily, wetting Baba to his last hair. If it were not for Beetle's condition, they would have had enjoyed the dolphin ride thoroughly. But each time the millipedes moved to adjust their grip on the floating hippos, Iora's heart sank. Baba arrived on the other side after the stretcher. Owlus and Iora came behind them, a little drier than Baba. With a bow from the hippos and a loud cheer from the Pink Dolphins, they went inside the jungle.

They couldn't climb the trees and take the branch

paths, which would have been faster in this area, owing to Beetle's stretcher. Iora and Owlus kept checking his eyes and were happy to observe them resume the natural colour. The jungle had become deep and dense again and it took their eyes a little time to adjust to the dim light.

"Agogwe camping site should be here somewhere. Keep looking for signs. It may be a few trees away and we may still miss it," said Baba.

Baba climbed the trees time and again to have a look around. Finally, he came down with information.

"Turn right," he said, "they are just a few paces away."

After a few minutes, they stood in the Agogwe settlement of semi-circular leaf huts. Little plump children played with monkeys, grown-ups carried on their daily chores, some just relaxed on hammocks and others dried meat and fish and cleaned yam and wild roots. Two young Agogwes played the guitar and bamboo flutes. It was their tradition to celebrate life as a long carnival by singing and dancing every day. They handled their musical instruments with tremendous care, for they were sacred to them.

The females had their long, black hair wrapped around their bodies neatly and so had the young males without beard. The elder ones had their beards wrapped around like Beetle. These little people looked a delightful lot. Baba entered first and most of them looked at him nonchalantly, taking him to be a passing ape. Then Iora and Owlus walked in with Beetle's stretcher. They all stood up in shock and a woman combing her little one's hair screamed. She ran towards Beetle and fell down on her knees.

"What has happened to him?" she asked, her eyes full of tears.

Baba put a hand on her shoulder and said comfortingly, "Do not worry; he will be fine in a couple of days. All he needs is rest."

Iora came forward and introduced herself, "You must be his wife, Mantis, and that must be your son, Dungy."

"Oh yes, he speaks a lot about his little friend. I've met your father, Heron; he's a wonderful Twitter. I thought we would meet in better circumstances . . ."

Beetle was placed by other Agogwes on a comfortable bed. The cheerful Agogwes were as pragmatic when it came to that.

"It is my mistake. If I had not told him what I'd set out to do, he wouldn't have come along," said Iora.

"Oh no, little dear. It is a noble thing you've set out to do. Bara, the *homo-avis* friend of Beetle, came after he'd guided you to the Wacky Wilderness from Twitterland. He told me about your mission and Beetle accompanying you," said Mantis.

"I am sure Beetle will recover soon. Healer Eelu had assured us . . ." said Owlus.

"I am sorry to interrupt, but we'll have to make a

move. We don't have much time," said Baba to Mantis. "And please don't worry. Beetle will be fine before you know it. He may be a little forgetful after he regains consciousness but that will be temporary."

"If you want someone to accompany you, any one of us would be glad to come along," said a young Agogwe, stepping forward.

"Thank you, young one. But we will manage."

Looking at Beetle for one last time, Iora and Owlus followed Baba out of the settlement. Iora was relaxed after leaving Beetle to the safety of his home. She knew he would be well taken care of. Owlus's colour returned to his cheeks.

"We will be in the Wacky Wilderness by nightfall. Just to keep you on alert, we may pass a dangerous area. Be prepared and gather these stones. This is the only area where we can get them," Baba said showing them greasy black stones bearing white dots.

But the stones were not scattered on the ground. There was a peculiar little plant with only one brown leaf. Baba showed how to pull it out. Every plant had one such stone tangled in its roots. After pulling out the stone the plants were to be placed again on their places and they immediately adjusted themselves by growing their roots, making firm their grip.

"Are we going to defend ourselves with these stones?" scoffed Owlus.

The stones were not easy to find but they managed

to get a handful each. They were not easy to carry either and kept slipping from their fingers, so Baba made two small vine bags for them to carry the stones. They had not got back their camouflage bags from Amazonland.

It was past noon when they entered an area where the jungle was not dense. Spiky rocks protruded from the ground like crocodiles' teeth. On top of each of these pointed rocks many flat rocks were balanced precariously.

"What is this place?" asked Owlus.

"Pass it quickly," said Baba.

His sense of hearing seemed to be excellent for quite some time now. Iora picked up something from the ground.

"Hey, there is a doll head. But it is so ugly. Yuck!" she exclaimed, holding a small shrunken head by its long, fuzzy hair.

"What kind of demented person would play with such a doll?" said Owlus, observing closely.

"Can we just leave it and move ahead?" asked Baba.

Iora shrugged looking at Owlus and hurried behind Baba. There was a rustling sound. They stopped to see pale, formidable-looking men and women around them – some hung straight or upside down on vines and branches and others emerged from behind the spiky rocks. They all were dressed in tatters of dried skin, most of which were frayed and dilapidated. Men and women had their hair tied back and the only ornament they wore was a garland of similar doll heads like the one Iora held. They had bow and arrows pointing towards the threesome.

What appeared like a young man came forward and smiled, revealing a set of badly decaying teeth.

"What am I supposed to do – hurl these stones at him?" Owlus asked Baba.

Iora looked at the repulsive doll head in her hand and those pierced in the garlands and a dreadful fact dawned on her, "These must be . . . the Head Hunters!"

18 The Head Hunters

"Trespassing, huh?" the young Head Hunter said in such a hoarse voice that it was indistinct; a shrunken head garland dangled from his ashen neck.

"A fat ape, a Twitter boy and . . . who are you girl?"

"I am a Twitter," said Iora, reacting in her usual bold manner when faced by frightful circumstances.

"An unlikely Twitter," commented a malicious-looking old woman hanging from a vine.

"Though I wouldn't eat her, I can gift her head to my little Huntress," said another man. "But her fat head will take long to shrink."

Iora's head swarmed and she couldn't think of any way out. The tribe had closed in on them from all sides. Owlus clutched his little bag of stones, prepared to attack with whatever he had. He had heard that Head Hunters were repulsed by fat and were very partial to thin people. He looked at Iora and Baba and realised both of them were not particularly thin except him. This clan followed cult of the dead and also believed that one can acquire virtues of others by digesting their bodies. Owlus shrank remembering his lessons.

Baba, who had the stones in his hands, slowly stretched out his fist and opened it to display the black and white stones.

"We just need to reach the Wacky Wilderness at the earliest. This is the shortest way across," said Baba.

All the Head Hunters lowered their bows and stared at the stones in Baba's hand. Seeing this, Iora too slowly took out the stones from her bag and held them in her palm. Owlus followed suit. Most of the Head Hunters just wanted to reach out and take those stones. But the young man who had come first raised his bow, gesturing them to stop. A dissonant clamour rose from the rest of the Head Hunters who looked mutinously at the young man for holding them back.

"What is so urgent, ape, that you put your heads on the line by crossing our area?" he asked.

"You can come and witness what we're trying to do on the moonless night at the Scar-faced River near Twitterland," answered Baba calmly. "It is for our collective good."

The young Head Hunter seemed bemused and kept staring at the three of them and the stones in turn. Finally, he lowered his bow. All the other Head Hunters looked with yearning at the stones.

They came towards the trio and two of them collected the stones from their extended palms, placing them tenderly on a flat rock. Owlus flinched at the touch of their splintered skin on his hands.

"Scat before we change our minds about unusual head trophies," said the young Head Hunter, who seemed to be their leader.

The three of them went away, leaving the group gathered around the flat rock.

"Phew! Now will anyone tell me what this was about?" said Owlus, once they were well out of earshot.

They had taken to the branch paths and followed Baba swinging on branches.

"We had to pass the Head Hunter territory. Those stones are a rare delicacy for them," informed Baba coming down on the branch path before them, scratching his hairy head with his long finger.

"They're going to *eat* those stones?" asked Iora.

"I can very well believe that seeing their state of teeth," said Owlus.

"Yes, Head Hunters are partial cannibals. But they also eat animals and vegetables and especially love this variety of rocks, which is actually a rare plant protein. Generally, they don't know where to find these rocks. They have feuds going on with many other tribes – mostly territorial disputes. That is why they are very touchy about trespassing."

"Yeah, one touchy lot!" said Owlus. "But why were those human heads so small?"

"They sever the heads of their enemies and boil and cool their heads repeatedly until they shrink in size. The more number of heads one has, the more heroic one is considered," said Baba.

"Beetle wouldn't have thought twice before bartering the shrunken heads with them," said Owlus.

"I hope he recovers soon . . ." sighed Iora.

Iora and Owlus continued asking questions about the Head Hunters. They found it fascinating. Baba's hearing went down and speed increased considerably.

"We have to reach the Wacky Wilderness before the evening falls," said Baba turning back to them. "Let's not try to waste any time."

"I certainly wouldn't like to waste time with the likes of Head Hunters," mumbled Owlus, who tried to keep pace with Iora.

They took shelter for a brief period only during the coffee time rain. By evening they were on the edge of the Wacky Wilderness.

"Now if there is no more hindrance we'll be inside the Wacky Wilderness in the early hours of the night," said Baba. "The woods become wackier as we proceed. So it is better to be at a safe place before the night creatures are at large," he said looking at Owlus who lagged far behind.

"I am sure you are aware that I didn't sleep properly

last night. I mean how could I, with Beetle lying like that by my side! I am tired and I can't hurry up!" said Owlus, who didn't seem impressed by Baba's indirect warning.

It was not dusk but it had become dark as usual. Iora and Baba had to halt again and again for Owlus.

A faint sob came from somewhere below, near the forest floor. Owlus heard it and halted but the sound stopped. Iora and Baba who were a little ahead didn't hear it.

"Now what is it?" Iora asked, tired and annoyed at Owlus stopping again. She stood a couple of trees away.

"Did you hear that sound?" he asked.

The only sounds audible were the croaks of frogs and chirping of crickets. They were so used to the night sounds that this was complete silence for them. Baba, who was in the lead, came back to Iora.

"What now?" he asked.

"I heard someone crying underneath," replied Owlus standing in attention.

"Now –" Iora began but stopped.

The muffled sobs were audible this time.

"What can that be?" asked Iora.

Owlus was energetic all of a sudden, and in a jiffy he came by Baba's side.

"It must be some hideous *Homo-lamia*," said Owlus, terrified.

"No, it is not a *Homo-lamia* or *Homo-malus*. It's a human voice," said Baba, listening intently.

"Who can it be, Baba, crying on the very edge of the Wacky Wilderness? The night has almost fallen," said Iora.

"It is a child's voice," said Baba matter-of-factly.

"Really!" exclaimed Iora.

Owlus was quite uninterested and itched to go away.

"It can be a Head Hunter, an Amazon or even a Twitter," said Iora. "We must go and find out."

"Oh sure, a Head Hunter kid! Oh boy, don't you remember what Baba himself said about trusting *no one*?" Owlus spluttered.

"But this does not smell dangerous," said Baba.

"This smells, tastes, looks and feels hazardous, perilous and treacherous to me!" said Owlus; the image of Beetle on the stretcher fresh in his head. "It can be some evil, no-gooder or some nasty, sweet-talking agent like that Sympathy Singer chap! Can't you see?"

"As much as I would have liked to continue, my instinct says this is someone in genuine trouble," said Baba. "You both wait here till I check and come."

"I will come along," said Iora.

"Okay," said Baba. The stifled sobs sounded as if someone was bidding a tired farewell to life. "But follow close behind and don't jump forward mindlessly. I would not advice you to stay alone, but you can stay if you wish," Baba said turning to Owlus.

"You bet I will!" said Owlus.

Baba quickly lit a couple of torches on two slow

burning twigs and handed one to Iora and the other to Owlus. Baba and Iora started to go down while Owlus looked on. As their sounds retreated, he raised his torch above his head. Darkness had engulfed the forest. Red and yellow pairs of eyes glowed of night animals and birds on prowl.

"Wait for me!" shouted Owlus, and went after them.

As they climbed down, the sobbing stopped. They looked around the jungle floor but except a few night animals, that looked at them inquisitively, nothing could be seen. Baba raised his hand and gestured them to remain where they were. Iora and Owlus stood still. Baba went around a wide tree and came back after a few moments. He gestured them to come and they approached, not knowing what to expect at the other side of the huge trunk. There sat, shivering, a little boy in strange frayed clothes, holding his legs folded close to his chest. Tears had made lines on his mud-coated face. He shrank from them, trying to squeeze in the tree trunk. Baba asked him who he was, but he shrank even further. Then, something seemed to dawn on him as he saw Iora.

"*I've seen you before*!" he said in an excited voice, which came out in a whisper.

19
The Lonely Wanderer

"What gibberish is he speaking?" muttered Owlus.

"Yes . . . I've seen him! I saw this boy the other day on the Scar-faced River . . . he's a non-jungle dweller!" Iora said, hot with excitement.

"Oh no! He must be dangerous! I told you both not to come here, didn't I?" squeaked Owlus.

"Can't you see he feels we are dangerous?" said Iora, and then added, looking at the boy in the same gibberish he had spoken, "*What are you doing here*?"

Owlus was taken aback and Baba seemed pleasantly surprised.

Before the boy could answer, Owlus said, "I know you can speak many jungle languages, but you speak non-jungly too, this is outrageous!"

"There is not one universal non-jungly language. There are many. I suppose Iora knows this one," said Baba.

"Yes, I also know a few words of other non-jungly languages. Father and Hoatzin have taught me," answered Iora.

"Are you for real?" spat Owlus.

"Incidentally, I know a little of what he's speaking," she replied.

"Can we argue later?" said Baba, and turned towards the frightened boy.

"I can speak some Jungly too," the boy whispered, and the three of them looked at him in shock.

"Who are you?" asked Baba, and waited patiently for him to start.

"I am Chinar. I came with my father and got lost in a storm. I cried, I shouted, I did everything to find my boat . . ." he said feebly and sat down.

"I've been walking for days but I can't find them." He started weeping.

Baba came near Chinar, put an arm around him, and said, "It's okay . . ."

"He must be hungry," said Iora.

"Do you want to eat something?" asked Baba.

Chinar nodded. He looked as if he hadn't eaten for days. "Water, please," he said faintly.

Baba cut a nearby vine and clear water flowed out of it. He got some in a leaf cup. Chinar had bruises all over his body. Blood dripped slowly from the wounds inflicted by leeches. Baba immediately got some leaves and lemur's saliva to apply over his wounds and also

Spitting Flower's pollen to reduce his pain.

"He's in a bad state," remarked Iora.

"He's in a very good state, Iora. A non-jungle dweller child lost in a rainforest and still alive for so many days! It is a marvel," replied Baba when he was done treating Chinar.

Baba then looked around. It was safe for him to leave the children and find some food for everyone. Once he left, Owlus came and poked Chinar with a finger to see what a non-jungle dweller felt like.

"What are you doing?" asked Iora.

"None of your business," he snapped.

They sat down at a little distance from Chinar. Chinar looked wretched with all his wounds, dishevelled hair and torn clothes. He observed them intently.

"Now, how do you know Jungly?" asked Iora.

"Are you all cannibals by any chance?" blurted Chinar.

"Of course! We're treating you so that you become healthy and we have a good meal. Is it not clear?" said Owlus.

Chinar seemed to turn paler in the light of the small fire they were all sitting around.

"Don't pay any heed to this nonsense, Chinar. Why do you think we would eat you?"

"I've heard stories of jungle people severing the heads of other people and cooking them," said Chinar and gulped, looking at the small fire.

“We’ve also heard a lot of stories about your lot. How you’re killing our jungles and how you want to wipe us out. We don’t come to your home and do that! Can’t you see we’re trying to help you out in spite of all this?” fumed Owlus.

Iora, for a change, agreed with Owlus.

She said, “Look, no one is going to harm you here. Now tell us, how do you know Jungly so well?”

“My father is a famous botanist. I mean, he studies plants. He comes regularly to the rainforests to collect specimens . . . samples for his research. But he has never been friendly with the inhabitants of the rainforest. I have been accompanying him since I was four years old. We always stay for a few days with Pygmies who live at the fringes of the rainforest. They are quite friendly . . .”

“Those traitors . . .” breathed Owlus.

“They are very kind! They bring a lot of new plants to my father. Papa gives them a lot of tobacco and other goodies on every trip. But he avoids any other jungle inhabitants. Except the Pygmies, the jungle people are not very friendly with us. I had once witnessed tall women attack our boat.”

“Must be our dear Amazons,” said Owlus.

“We always stay at the Pygmy village. I play with pygmy kids so I picked up this language there. They say I have a very good knack for languages.”

“What an undesirable trait!” said Owlus, looking at Iora.

"But I had no idea that monkeys could speak Jungly as well . . ." Chinar said looking in the direction where Baba had gone.

Owlus started laughing hysterically and Iora tried to control her laughter.

She cleared her throat and said, "It's like this, Chinar – Jungly is understood by many jungle creatures. Jungle tribes and creatures have their own language, but this is a common tongue, which is understood by many, including plants and trees in some areas. There are creatures who do not understand it and you've to learn their language to speak to them."

"I know Jungly but still have never spoken to animals, leave alone trees!" said Chinar.

Everyone became quiet for some time.

Chinar broke the silence, "Father says that jungle people are not to be trusted. I don't agree, you know! But he feels they are always spinning yarns about fantastical creatures to misguide us."

"Oh yes, we have nothing better to do!" Owlus snapped.

Baba returned with an armload of things to eat. He quickly prepared the meal and gave special medicinal victuals to Chinar; he refrained from informing that they contained Tricky Toad's toes and mottled wings of Dingy Dragonflies. Chinar stuffed so much food in his mouth that they thought he'd choke. This was new kind of food, which he'd not tasted even on his stays with the Pygmies. He seemed to like it quite a bit.

After dinner, Baba said, “We will have to take him along with us.”

All the three were taken aback alike.

“You must be joking!” said Owlus.

“Our speed will slow down!” joined Iora.

“I thought you would help me get back to my boat,” said Chinar, losing hope.

“See, little ones, we do not know where his boat is. From what I understand, it is beyond Twitterland. It is at least six to seven days’ walk from here. We do not have this much time, and chances of his people being at the same place all these days are bleak. We cannot leave this boy here to die, can we?” he said to Iora and Owlus, and then turned to Chinar, “I know this may sound very harsh, little one, but we are not even sure if your people are still there, and if they are, then where.”

Iora thought for a while and said, “You are right, Baba. We should take him along. We cannot leave him at the verge of the Wacky Wilderness.”

“We will help him keep pace with us,” said Baba.

“Yeah, all right. Take him along. If nothing else, I will come to know more about their funny tribe,” said Owlus.

Baba patted Iora and Owlus with his hairy hand.

But Chinar was still shocked. “Where are you going to take me? Maybe my father has stopped looking for me, but I will find a way back to him. I must! I will build a boat and cross the sea to go back to my mother . . .” he said with watery eyes.

"What a brilliant plan!" said Owlus. Baba warned him with a look.

"We are on an extremely important mission, Chinar. Otherwise we would have tried our best to find your people right away. But the future of this forest depends on certain things to be done before the next moonless night," said Iora.

"We may come to the sea or even pass the Scar-faced River again in a few days. But you must not be left here alone," said Baba kindly.

Chinar looked around the obscure forest shadows in the flickering fire and shuddered, hearing squeaks and hollers. He had barely survived since he was lost and this was a blessing of sorts. He felt safe in this unusual company.

Chinar slept like a baby in the shelter made by Baba. The next morning, when he woke up, it took him some time to put the pieces in place – a boy and a girl almost of his age sleeping besides him and a large orangutan preparing breakfast. He felt rejuvenated and remembered the delicious dinner. Baba's medicine had done wonders to his wounds.

"Now, what you need is a good breakfast," said Baba, looking at Chinar.

Iora and Owlus also got up, yawning. Chinar felt grateful. The last night he didn't know if he would be alive the next morning.

He saw one scaly anteater come happily towards

them and lick his breakfast with its long, sticky tongue. He backed up startled. Owlus snorted.

"Don't worry, Chinar. You should've seen the palm civet which lay sleeping on Owlus's lap one morning!" informed Iora. Owlus stopped laughing.

There were fresh clothes made of leaves and bark placed near Chinar.

"Wear this. I can see mushrooms growing out of your moist clothes," said Baba.

He changed into the new clothes and shoes.

"Why were you wearing so many clothes in the jungle?" asked Iora, surprised at the ignorance of non-jungle dwellers who didn't know they had to wear bare minimum in a rainforest.

They started again, on ground this time, to make it easier for Chinar. They had not entered the Wacky Wilderness as yet, which they were supposed to the previous night. But in spite of the delay, Baba seemed smitten with a fit of laziness, even after crossing the threshold of the Wacky Wilderness. He sniffed twigs, closely watched the soil, checked the direction of the wind, climbed the tree canopy and came down again, checked the moisture in the air with the help of spongy Wish-Weather Worms, combed his long, unkempt hair with Comb Cocoons and did other unnecessary things. Iora and Owlus knew him well by now, and understood he was going to proceed at his own pace. They got busy with Chinar who was full of inquiries himself. When they had explained to him who they were and what their mission was, Chinar looked at them disbelievingly. They started asking him about his world and it was their turn to look unconvinced.

"Father says jungle people are frozen in time since the Stone Age. They have a timeless culture. They are ruled by the law of the jungle, that is, they have no law at all!" said Chinar and added, "But this is not what I think."

"Is he talking about *us*?" asked Owlus, his anger rising.

"I do not believe in it. I love the jungles. I really do!" said a scared Chinar.

Before Iora or Chinar could reply, Baba stopped. Turning to Chinar, he said, "The Law of the Jungle is that that the mighty sustains the weak, nothing goes waste in nature and animals kill only for sustenance and not for greed. Cruelty is not the Law of the Jungle, little one."

"I didn't mean that! But I am sorry if I offended you," said Chinar, realising that if what his father had told him was correct, these creatures wouldn't be helping him.

They came across a small stream falling from a rock and Chinar requested if he could take a quick bath. Baba consented and he went down the sprinkling waterfall. They could see his face much more clearly now. He had a wheatish skin, sharp features and black, wavy hair, which he arranged with his fingers. A deep dimple appeared on his right cheek when he smiled which particularly interested Owlus.

"Deformed face," he commented.

When they climbed the trees again with Baba helping Chinar to walk on the branch paths, Owlus turned to Iora and said, "He looks like a compulsive liar to me. Flying on non-living objects, a box which plays music and tells stories, phone – on which you can talk from one end of the forest to the other. Does he think we are fools?"

"His non-jungle world would be full of dark anti-natural things. Or else he is really imaginative to make all that up," said Iora.

Chinar was so thrilled walking on trees, seeing different creatures and talking to the large ape, Baba, that he quite forgot he was lost. Finally, around noon, Baba stopped and asked them to climb down.

"Early lunch I guess," said Owlus, landing with a thud on the jungle floor.

"Shhhhh . . ." said Baba.

They stood silently as Baba looked around the place.

"I must be mistaken," he said after a while and told them to climb up again when a weather beaten rock with many cracks in it stirred. It was inclined on a tree's roots, which had grown amok above the ground.

Its cracks formed a mouth and said, "Here, Baba. Go a little ahead in the northeast. If you climb back you wouldn't be able to find it."

"Thank you, there. I owe you one," said Baba to the rock.

"A talking rock!" muttered Chinar. "You didn't tell me that rocks talk as well!"

"If we had ever been told, we would have certainly told you!" said Iora and looked towards a highly amused Owlus.

"A talking rock, how neat is that! Let's take a piece of it!" said Owlus.

"Remember when you tried to take a singing frog along?" asked Iora.

Owlus turned red in the face; hot guilt shot through his insides, remembering Beetle on the fur stretcher.

The talking rock chuckled. Iora and Owlus speedily followed Baba who had gone in the northeast direction.

They had hardly walked a few paces when the ground shivered for a moment. They stopped and it shivered again, as if hit by a mild earthquake. The trembling of the forest floor increased.

"Shouldn't we run?" Owlus asked Baba, pulling his long hair.

Before Baba could reply, a giant talon came into view advancing from behind a tree. A huge bird with solid legs and intimidating talons, a thin, long neck holding a wizened face with a large, flashy silver beak and another identical face on its abdomen emerged. The second thing they noticed after this bird was an eagle, big enough to kill a jaguar and fly with it in its beak, sitting high above in the middle layers of the trees. Iora wondered how it could come below the thick canopy with its massive wingspan. A couple of sparrows followed the giant two-headed bird and perched on some branches above.

"Baba," said the bird in a thundering voice, "you have come to see me."

The crooked-beaked eagle high above had bent its head down to observe the four creatures closely.

"Bird Angel, I am honoured beyond words that you grace me with your presence again," said Baba, going down on his knees.

"Rise, Baba. You know I do not like this paying respect business just as you don't like being addressed as 'Sir'," said the Angel, smiling.

Baba smiled and said, "I am highly honoured that you remember this little detail about a humble creature."

Chinar seemed in a trance and Iora and Owlus went down on their knees.

"You know I am a nomad and do not live in a particular abode to avoid followers around me. I love the jungle and just do my job. Scorpo did a smart thing by sending you to find me. I couldn't have counted on anyone but you to locate me, barring my eagle of course."

Baba, who had stood up, bowed again.

"You a-a-are the Bird Angel? I was always told it was a paradise bird!" said Owlus, torn between wonder and bewilderment.

"I knew . . . I mean Father had told me that the Bird Angel was not a paradise bird," said Iora, looking at the Bird Angel with awe.

"My father, or no one else for that matter, told me none of this!" said Chinar, thrilled and pinching himself to see if it was true.

Thunderbird, the Bird Angel, looked at Baba and said, "So you've taken upon yourself to see through this crisis the jungle is facing."

"I am just trying to protect these children from the dark anti-natural forces. Otherwise it is entirely their effort."

"Will you turn around?"

Baba turned around but the Angel did not look in his direction, rather she raised her head and looked at the sky that was not visible. She looked back at Baba and chirped a pleasant note. One of the two sparrows flew down and sat on Baba's back. It raised Baba's long tresses with its beak and everyone saw deep gashes beneath. Iora and Owlus looked shocked at the sight.

"You've been taking on the agents of the anti-natural forces all alone? At least take a little care of yourself, fearless one," said the Angel.

"But when did this happen?" asked Iora in a shaky voice.

"I am sure it has been happening in the late hours of night when you are asleep. Those forces are the most powerful then," said the Angel.

"But he's badly hurt, we can't proceed like this!" said Owlus.

"Oh no, I am absolutely fine!" protested Baba.

The Angel spread her wings and flapped them a couple of times. The sparrow flew away from Baba's back. A roaring sound and a distant rumbling of thunder were heard. It seemed the coffee time rain was about to pour in early today. The jungle turned darker, indicating that there were clouds overhead. Without another warning note, rain came down in a surge.

"Come beneath my wings," said the Angel to all of them, spreading her wings.

Baba, Owlus, Iora and Chinar quickly came and stood below the wide spread of wings.

"Baba, you come beneath my right wing," instructed the Angel and he followed her command, leaving the rest of them standing beneath the left wing, fully protected from the rain.

However, this wing, beneath which Baba stood, seemed porous and some raindrops filtered from it and fell on him. After a few moments, she began to lower her wings.

"Hey, this wing is going to close in on us!" shrieked Owlus.

All of them looked up to see a giant wing closing in on them but it furled just above their heads. The rain stopped abruptly.

"Did you think I was going to hurt you, Owlus?" said the bird's second head on the abdomen.

"No, of course not, Angel. It's just that it was so sudden . . ." answered Owlus, flushing.

The sparrow flew and sat on Baba's back again, lifting his long hair with its beak. There were no wounds or deep gashes there. All the lesions had vanished.

"I couldn't thank you enough, Angel!" said Baba, bowing gratefully.

"Wow!" muttered Owlus.

"So, Iora," said Thunderbird, stepping ahead, "is it going to be the Scar-faced River near Twitterland?"

"Yes, my Angel," answered Iora. "You wouldn't believe how thrilled the Twitters would be to see their own Angel face to face! Most of them think they can never see you in their lifetimes."

"I am sure your father does not believe so," said Thunderbird.

Iora smiled and said, "Yes, my Angel, he has always believed he would meet you one day."

"Now you all should get going. I could have offered some help but till the time you have Baba to help you, there is nothing to worry," chirped Thunderbird, glancing towards the Sparrows and Eagle bird spirits.

"But, Angel, we have not found the Spirit of the Jungle as yet. Can you please help us out? You are our own Angel and you know our lives depend on finding it," said Owlus.

"It is for those to find out, who've taken up this noble task," answered Thunderbird.

"But we don't know . . . we're clueless!" implored Owlus.

"No one in this world is all knowing, neither demons nor angels," replied Thunderbird.

She smiled behind her heavy blue beak.

Owlus looked disappointed but bowed nevertheless in acceptance. Chinar kept staring at her other head on the abdomen.

"We will take your leave, my Angel," said Baba, and all of them bowed, including Chinar who didn't want all this to end. When they raised their heads there was nothing around. Thunderbird along with her bird spirits, the giant eagle and the two sparrows, had gone.

Iora turned towards Baba and said, "Baba, you've been fighting all alone and you've not even breathed a word about it!"

"Yes, you should've told us. With those wounds how far do you think you could have taken us? We have a right to be kept informed," joined Owlus.

It seemed Baba's hearing had weakened again. He got engrossed in doing some calculations and drawing a map on the wet ground with a stick. Owlus looked at Iora and shrugged his shoulders, "Useless to talk to him!"

"This is so frustrating!" said Iora.

"Yes, that's right," said Baba, still looking down, "we'll first go to the Aqua Angel and then to the Tree Angel, as their abodes are the nearest to Twitterland.

We'd still be far from Twitterland. I'll have to take the shortest cut to get you back there within time."

He then looked up at the three of them and said, "I've estimated the travelling time assuming all goes well. We have only nine days to go. You are well aware that the anti-natural forces are behind us. So little ones, needless to say that time is something we can't waste. This is to keep you informed," he concluded, looking at Owlus.

"Why do I get a feeling that there is nothing wrong with his hearing?" Owlus whispered.

20
The Rock and the Croc

Baba began moving faster than before. The terrain became increasingly difficult, the creatures more unfriendly, and the woods deeper. Even the gentle grazing herds of deer seemed ready to attack. But some creatures knew Baba and he possessed a most extraordinary way to deal with hostile creatures he chanced upon. But mostly, he avoided getting in the way of any. Owlus and Iora followed him alertly. It was Chinar who was most thrilled in spite of being the most unfamiliar with even the existence of such places. He could have hardly climbed a tree or avoided a stinging bee had it not been Baba taking his hand and helping him after every two steps. But this did not slow Baba's pace. He would swing Chinar by taking his hand and place him ahead of himself. Chinar had to barely carry his own weight and he quite forgot all his misery in this fairy tale land.

"No one is going to believe me back home! Talking monkeys, two-headed giant birds, Twitters . . . I must write a book named 'Chinar in Wonderland'. Or should I name it 'Charzan of Apes'?" he said, looking at Baba.

"I think I liked him better when he was depressed," said Owlus.

"You told me all about the Meeting of Five and your friend Beetle. Please tell me something about the Bird Angel," Chinar requested Owlus.

"Oh well, since my not telling you wouldn't shut you up, it would be better that I hear my own voice," said Owlus, rather pleased. "Thunderbird is a very powerful Angel in the cosmos of the jungle. She is the hope with feathers – the hope of the jungle that forever flies. She waters the earth by bringing the rain and helping mighty trees grow. The beating of her wings rolls the thunder and lightning flashes from her silver beak. Bird spirits – the giant eagle and the two sparrows – accompany her."

By early evening, they reached the top of a mountain, which Iora had thought she couldn't have climbed in three days. Thanks to Baba's shortcuts. A faint roaring sound became audible.

"What is that sound?" asked Owlus in apprehension.

"No idea . . . let's ask Baba."

Baba was a little ahead of them, climbing towards the canopy and helping Chinar along.

Both of them reached the canopy after Baba and

Chinar. Before they could ask him about the sound, they were dumbstruck to see what lay before them.

The thick green of the jungle covered the mountain range on one side, and on the other it seemed the mountain range had been sliced into a semi-circular half. There was a steep rocky drop and right below spread the endless expanse of the azure sea. Sun rested peacefully on the rim of the watery horizon. Waves crashed headlong on the rocks, which were wedged between the rocky mountains and sea, in a regular rhythm.

"Sea!" muttered Chinar holding Owlus's hand to balance himself on the treetop.

Owlus didn't mind as he was too gripped by the scene that extended before him.

"It is so big . . . and growls constantly!" said Iora, spellbound.

"I thought you both may have not seen it, so I climbed up here," said Baba.

That was right; Iora and Owlus had never seen a sea in their lives, and it took them a little time to comprehend its vastness.

"Father always said he'll bring me to the sea when I grow up . . ." said Iora. She had a very strong urge to be with her father.

"My father had also once seen it and he doesn't stop talking about it when the topic crops up," said Owlus.

It was dusk and the sun slowly drowned in the sea.

"I've never seen the sun go down in the water before.

Always seen it go down the trees or hills," said Owlus with a distant look.

The sky changed from pink to fiery red to ashy crimson – the colour of dying cinders. They watched it peacefully for some time. Baba got up to get going.

"I hope we don't have to climb down that nerve-racking rock face," said Owlus.

"No, we don't have to go to the sea," replied Baba. "We will take the other route down and cover a little more distance before calling it a day."

They climbed down the middle layers of the trees and resumed walking on the branch paths. It got dark. Baba lit two torches for Owlus and Iora. He wanted to keep both of Chinar's hands free so that he could assist himself.

"I just didn't feel like moving away from there. The sound of the waves was musical," said Iora.

"Yes, it seems it is their job to keep rising with the wind and crashing on the rocks. What a life . . . Did you see how steep that cliff was? And you've been sailing in the sea you say?" said Owlus, turning to Chinar.

Owlus stopped as he saw the devastated look on Chinar's face through the light of his torch.

"Did you see a *Homo-lamia*?" asked Owlus.

"What's wrong, Chinar?" asked Baba, who also stopped.

"The sea . . ." Chinar stammered, fighting back tears. "My folks might be sailing on it somewhere right now, heading homewards . . . Will I ever meet them again . . .?"

Even Owlus felt bad for him. Seeing the enormity of the ocean firsthand, Iora and Owlus had serious doubts if Chinar would ever be able to make it back home alone, if his people had already left.

"Don't worry, little one. After all this is over, we'll figure something out," said Baba softly.

"Yes, don't lose heart, Chinar. We're here with you," said Iora.

Owlus also nodded in consent. They all began walking silently. Homesickness had rubbed off on Iora and Owlus. Thoughts of home weighed heavy in Iora's mind. Owlus's head was clouded with memories, which seemed so distant. But both distracted themselves by helping Chinar to learn and adapt to the rainforest.

The woods got more perilous as the moon thinned each night with the approach of the moonless night. As the Animal Angel became weaker, the dark anti-natural forces gained power. Baba tried his best not to leave them alone, especially Iora. He could sense dark agents lurking around all the time, but not coming forth for fear of him. Tonight, they had to be content with grapefruits and taro roots, as Baba couldn't leave them for long intervals to fetch food.

Next morning they started early. Chinar was still not in the best of spirits. Animal traffic was high during the early morning hours. Night animals retreated and morning animals came out. The animals generally didn't leave their set paths. They could always get in trouble, walking on narrow branches. So they descended on the jungle floor where they could move aside to give way to the passing animals.

"Now I should tell you not to show a lot of inquisitiveness around here," said Baba. "You may find strange things in this area but it would be wise to keep away and not touch anything."

"You mean like this strange hole here?" asked Owlus, touching a small tapering formation on the ground with his stick.

As soon as the stick touched it, it made an exploding sound and sizzling red-hot liquid came out of it in a gush. It stopped as quickly, emitting a small mushroom-shaped cloud of smoke. They all looked in wonder at the hot liquid spilled around.

"That's exactly what I meant," said Baba with a sigh. "Don't touch anything unusual."

They started again and found many such small hill-shaped protrusions.

"But what are these, Baba?" asked Iora.

"These are tiny volcanoes which go off on touch. So imagine if it was your finger instead of the stick."

While going downhill they came across many weird things and creatures the whole day. This had a cheering effect on Chinar. He felt particularly interested in a massive three-feet long flower with thick purple, yellow and red petals.

"That is Devil's Beetle Box. I would not venture into

sitting on it if I were you," said Baba, who saw Chinar attempting to climb onto it.

Iora and Owlus didn't find it harmful to touch things around with their sticks until a one-eyed, one-legged red and yellow Macaw, whom Owlus poked with his stick, came hopping angrily opening its beak and exposing a set of sharp teeth.

The rest of the day and night passed uneventfully if we do not consider Iora stepping on the fire farting ant, Owlus plucking a berry which had a tubular mouth that threw bad breath all over the would-be consumer, Chinar holding a vine to balance himself which turned out to be a green pit viper and Baba trying to do crisis management.

The next morning they started a little late as Owlus had come up with a new problem. He wanted to drink woodapple nectar. It was not until Baba had made it and he drank it to his heart's delight that they started again. Iora was very cross with him and spoke only to Chinar. By afternoon they reached a wide valley. They had to go to the other side and climb another mountain. There was only one trouble – the valley was a large swamp.

Half-submerged slender marsh trees intercepted it, but they could not cross the swamp on branch paths, as the trees were thin and placed away from each other. The swamp was quite muddy at places and Baba knew if someone once starts to sink in, there is no coming out. They stood there, silently listening to the croaking of frogs and small sloshes, splashes and splatters in the marsh. The light was dim and there was hardly any movement around. Baba thought hard but couldn't come up with any immediate solution to cross it.

"Reluctant as I am to leave you alone, I find no other way but to go and arrange for a transport. We must cross before sundown. If you all promise to not try anything funny, I will come back in no time. So?" asked Baba.

"Oh yes, I'll take care of both of them. Don't worry old chum and come back soon so that we pass this place as soon as possible," said Owlus glancing around the stillness and gloom. He was in a fidgety mood since morning and had become more edgy standing in front of the ominous swamp.

"Yeah, right!" exclaimed Iora, "I will make sure Owlus takes care of us."

"I will be back soon," assured Baba. "Do not go near the swamp," he commanded and took off.

"I will take a short walk on the side of the swamp," said Owlus getting fidgety.

"Yeah, let's do that," said Iora.

"But we shouldn't go out of the way," said Chinar.

The trio moved on the bank of the swamp.

"Hey, what's that?" said Iora pointing at a series of flat rocks laid a step away from each other in the swamp and leading right up to the other end.

"Interesting . . ." said Owlus, and after observing them for a while said, "We can easily cross from here."

"Oh no, no, no! Don't you remember what Baba said? No funny business!" said Chinar.

"Yes, we are in enough trouble already. You don't want us to get into a new one, Mr Guardian?" said Iora.

"It is a piece of cake! These rocks are so neatly arranged. Leave aside dangerous creature, there is not even a normal one in sight except frogs," said Owlus.

"Have you forgotten the experience with that frog?"

"Oh come on, Iora, I wouldn't be talking to any frogs. I just want to get out of this place. It's giving me the creeps!" said Owlus. "Anyway, Baba is still not back and I bet he would be happy to see us on the other side without his aid."

"It is a bad idea, Owlus," said Iora.

"These rocks don't seem slippery. I can at least go a little ahead and see. Otherwise I will turn back," said Owlus.

Before Iora or Chinar could convince him otherwise, he ran to the swamp and placed a foot on the flat stone, which was nearest to the bank.

"See, it is alright. I will go a little ahead." He stepped on the next stone.

"Wait, don't be silly! Come back right away!" shouted Iora, stretching out her hand to him.

But Owlus went humming ahead, placing carefully one foot at a time from one stone to the next.

"All the stones are not even, Owlus! Can't you see

there are some uneven ones here and there? What if there is slippery moss on it?" said Iora.

"This is crazy!" said Chinar shaking his head.

"I'll manage easily," said Owlus, who was in the middle of the swamp by now. He carefully stepped on an uneven stone. It shook a little.

"Oh, it is slippery!" Chinar trembled.

"Get away from that stone! Pronto!" hollered Iora.

Owlus lost all his confidence and tried to balance himself to step onto the next stone. But before he could do that, the uneven stone under him started emerging from the water.

"It is a marsh crocodile's back!" said Iora looking at Chinar who stood gaping in terror, wiping his sweating hands on his leafy clothes.

The massive crocodile emerged and Owlus slipped. He landed flat on its thorny uneven back.

"Get its eyes, Owlus! Get its eyes!" screamed Iora.

She herself stepped on the nearest stone in the marsh and jumped from one stone to the other to reach the vigorously shaking crocodile with Owlus on its back. She realised he could not possibly free his hands to reach the crocodile's eyes as it would throw him into the swamp. The waters had turned muddy due to the struggle.

Chinar stood on the bank, transfixed. As if waking from a reverie, he shouted, "I am also coming!"

"No, you are not!" said Iora turning around towards Chinar on the bank.

"Watch your back, Iora!" bellowed Chinar so loudly that even the indifferent frogs and crickets stopped croaking and chirping.

Iora turned abruptly to see a large open mouth, with jagged teeth and a thick pink tongue, about to catch her head. She gasped but without wasting one split second she turned and jumped on the next stone and the next. Within moments, she was on the bank near Chinar with the large crocodile in hot pursuit. The croc came on the bank behind her. By then both Iora and Chinar had already run a little away towards the woods. It stopped and turned its bulky self to the easy prey struggling in the swamp.

21 The Swamp

With amazing determination, Owlus still held onto the back of the frantically moving crocodile. Iora came running towards the bank again, followed by Chinar. To their horror, they saw a dozen more marsh crocodiles surfacing near Owlus to get a mouthful of meat.

"Somebody help! Oh Baba, where are you . . ." muttered Iora, turning red in the face and looking around for some way to help.

Owlus had begun to lose the grip. He was so exhausted that he had even stopped shouting for help. The crocodiles had already started fighting for their share. Iora had to act. She stepped on a flat stone near the bank to go towards Owlus, when something caught the corner of her eye. She looked in that direction but there was nothing. Again there was a movement and this time she saw a lump of mud land right on top of the raging crocodiles. Before the crocodiles, Iora or Chinar could make out what was going on, they saw the lump jump away, holding Owlus.

It took the crocodiles a moment or two to figure out what had just happened. Meanwhile, the muddy form swam away at a fast pace, holding Owlus above water. Iora and Chinar ran on the bank side with it. It seemed Owlus was floating on the water on his back all by himself. He was knocked out and limp and a dozen crocodiles followed close behind. They would not give up so easily. One crocodile swam ahead of the others, gained on Owlus, and snapped its jaws. Its snout grazed on Owlus's limp feet.

Just then, something whizzed past in the air. Before the crocodile in the lead could snap again, it turned upside down exposing its pale yellow stomach. The whizzing sound came again and another croc writhed with pain. The rest of the crocodiles slowed their pace and gradually stopped following.

"What's happening?" asked Chinar between breaths.

Iora didn't reply. She looked intently at the swamp trees while running. She thought she spotted something but it did not make sense to halt. What if these creatures had rescued Owlus for their own meal?

Owlus's speed slowed down and he floated towards the shore. He was gently pushed on land. A human form, covered fully in mud, surfaced after Owlus. He had two large, mismatched magenta eyes with no nose and was soaked to his last hair in mud. He stood there, bent and puffing, while Iora approached him cautiously. On a closer look, she realised that he was not covered with mud, but actually had a mud-textured skin. It seemed he breathed through his skin.

"Hey, thanks for saving him," she said, as she couldn't think of anything better to begin the conversation.

Owlus lay moaning and swearing in his unconscious state. Chinar arrived after Iora. Before they could reach Owlus, three more creatures, two small and one almost the same size as the first one, emerged from the swamp. The last one, carrying a sharp pointed stick in its hands, went straight to Owlus and felt his face. This one looked like a female. The creatures' bright magenta, mismatched eyes made quite a contrast to their muddy skin. They seemed naked on the first look. But on a closer observation, one could see their grubby clothes made out of a thin layer of mud, looking like an extension of their skins. The two little ones stared at Owlus, Iora and Chinar in turns. She could detect this with the movement of their heads as their eyes pointed elsewhere. A thin, translucent film flickered on their eyes every few seconds. They had large splayed feet and hands, the fingers connected with a thin film of skin.

"Who are you?" Iora asked anxiously.

The female who was bent near Owlus mumbled something to the other creature.

"Krrrr. Come along," said the first creature, and

without any notice all the four mud creatures jumped in the swamp again, carrying Owlus above water.

Iora and Chinar glanced at each other and ran down the swamp again by their side. The creatures didn't take Owlus further inside the swamp but swam besides the bank avoiding the slender trees.

Finally, they slowed down their pace and Iora and Chinar saw a strange city in the swamp. It had huts with conical thatched roofs, half submerged in water. Many mud creatures darted in and out of the huts. The marsh was quite wide here and a thin mist hung over it. Mud creatures were perched on large lily leaves and the rooftops of the huts. Some of them were adorned with shells and fish scales. They looked as amused seeing the three children as Iora and Chinar were on seeing them. Owlus was placed on a lily leaf and some creatures swam towards him. The female rubbed a few lily petals and mud together and applied it on his forehead.

Chinar sat wheezing on a root. Iora stood panting near the bank. The four creatures that had rescued Owlus saw her and came ashore.

"He is fine. Krrrrrrrk. Just shocked, nothing else."

He made a strange noise while speaking which sounded somewhere between a child's giggle and frog's croak. Both his eyes looked in different directions.

"Thank you very much. But who are you and why did you save him?" asked Iora.

Before he could answer, a large mud creature, trailed

by two others, came floating near them. He came on the ground and stood straight in front of the four creatures.

"Why Krrrrrrrk meddlesome Gud-gud family will never learn!" he said in a soft, subtle voice. Two other creatures that trailed behind him nodded in agreement.

The other creatures examining Chinar also turned towards the bank.

"Krrrrrrrk. We had no choice. We krrrrrrrk didn't interfere till the last moment. Crocs would have shred this boy krrrrrrk to pieces had my family not stopped them with poison darts krrrk kit kit," said Gud-gud.

"Do you expect a pat on your back? It would have been good if this boy was krrrrrrrrk consumed by the crocs. The crocs would have been krrrrrrrrk peaceful for a while," said the large creature in a subtler voice than before, squinting his magenta eyes at Owlus.

The female standing by Gud-gud's side started to say something but a shriek stopped her. They looked in Owlus's direction. He sat on the large leaf surrounded by the mud creatures. He had a look on his face of one who has awoken from a nightmare to see that reality was worse.

"It's okay, Owlus. These kind people have saved you," said Iora from the shore, not sure if she was right.

Not able to contain himself, Owlus said, "Don't you think these guys need a bath?"

The large creature smiled more coldly than ever and turned to Gud-gud. "So this is the Krrrrrrrk innocent boy you saved. If we have been Krrrrrrk compromised one bit today, we all know who is to be blamed."

The two creatures standing behind him looked ferociously at Gud-gud with their aimless eyes.

"There is no danger we bring you, kind people," began Iora, "we are in fact indebted to you."

Chinar slowly approached Iora and stood by her side.

"You must be wondering Krrrrrk who we are," said the female. "Krrrrrrrk. We are *Homo-aquaticus*. You can call us Pebbles. My husband Gud-gud and our two children spotted you in danger. But what are you doing here?"

Iora told the attentive lot the story in brief. As she finished she heard a familiar growl.

"You could have given my old heart a severe attack!" Baba said, advancing towards them.

Along with him was an insect, five times taller than Baba, with six thin unbalanced legs carrying a flat body on the top, stumbling behind. Its bottle-green flat head bore two small eyes, hardly visible from below. Its flat mouth with two cutter semi-circular appendages opened and closed every few seconds but no sound came out of it. Everyone looked at the insect with interest. Iora half wanted to greet it but sensing Baba's mood she stopped.

"You wouldn't believe what happened, Baba," Iora started.

"I think one of you . . . Owlus," said Baba, looking at him seated on the oversized lily leaf, "messed up with the marsh crocodiles and was saved by Pebbles. I know about children's curiosity, but this is too much!"

Iora wanted to complain about Owlus but kept quiet.

"So it is the great Baba Krrrrrk," croaked the hostile creature softly, "on another bizarre mission. Whatever this girl is saying Krrrrrrrk . . . you keep us out of this mess!"

Baba ignored him and turned towards Gud-gud and family, whom his seasoned eyes had spotted as Owlus's saviours, and said, "I thank you for your help."

"Krrrrrk. Oh no, great Baba, you don't have to thank us! We've heard Krrrrrk so much about you. In fact, we are glad to help these children who're up to such a remarkable task," said Gud-gud.

Some Pebbles pushed Owlus's leaf to the bank.

"Shall we? Daddy Long Legs has other work to do as well," said Baba, looking at the insect.

Gud-gud's two children came running to Baba and held his hands. "Krrrrrrrrk. We've Krrrrr heard your stories, Baba! Can't you stay?"

"Some other time, little ones. Right now we are in a hurry," said Baba patting their heads.

"Can't we request Pebbles to help us cross?" asked Iora.

"We can cross from here, but we will not come out at the right place. And can't put Pebbles in any more trouble," said Baba.

Iora cast a last look at the gloomy village of Pebbles

and moved forward, waving goodbye to the Gud-gud family. Owlus still wobbled on his feet when they were out of sight of the colony. Chinar gave him a hand time and again but Owlus refused to take it. He had set out to make a big impression by crossing the swamp all on his own and ended up making a show of himself. He was annoyed and instead of being quiet, he had become more boisterous. Iora turned a cold shoulder to him and Baba, though upset because of all this waste of time, maintained his cool.

Daddy Long Legs was the silent kinds. He minded his flat head and abdomen, suspended high above the ground, from the tree branches, squinting his small eyes further. Baba stopped at a place where the swamp squeezed into a tapered strip. Chinar spotted something slither by in the waters but could not see it clearly. It seemed for a split second that the creature turned its head and gave him a malicious smile.

All this adventure is taking its toll on my head, he thought.

Baba turned to Daddy Long Legs. "This is it. We must cross from here."

Daddy Long Legs came to a fumbled halt and sat down by turning and bending his legs at extreme angles.

"And what is the guarantee that he wouldn't drop us in the middle of the marsh?" demanded Owlus.

"I can tell you he is more reliable than the rocks you tried to cross on," answered Baba, "and you must go first."

Owlus stared at the insect in disgust. Seeing no use in pushing his luck further with Baba, he climbed on the hairy back of the insect.

Daddy Long Legs stood up, oscillating on his unsteady legs, and Owlus would have fallen flat on his face had he not held on to his squishy abdomen tightly. He entered the swamp with Owlus clutching his back. They progressed in the bog and his extended legs submerged more and more. He did not wobble as before and walked steadily. Owlus breathed a sigh of relief when he crossed the bog and sat down clumsily like a boiled potato falling on the ground.

"Stand right there till we reach, Owlus," shouted Baba from the other side.

Chinar rode the insect this time. He was deposited safely on the other side.

"So much better than the last amusement park I've been to!" he told Owlus.

The insect crossed to the other side and sat down in his slouched potato manner. It was now Iora's turn to climb.

"Hold on very tight," said Baba.

The insect's legs sank deeper and deeper as they progressed in the swamp. They were midway when he jerked a little.

"What's wrong?" Iora asked.

She could see a part of his legs above the water, but couldn't see below it, as the water was murky. He jerked again and this time Iora saw a scaly swamp serpent trying to reach the insect's abdomen. Or was it trying to reach her, she wondered. She could see the thick back of the serpent bearing a diamond-shaped pattern. The diamond shapes bore all the rainbow colours and as it moved around the half-submerged legs, it looked like a twisted rainbow.

"Baba!" she cried.

"Just hold on tight!" Baba cried anxiously from the shore.

Iora saw the scaly creature try in vain to coil around the slippery thin legs. She realised the strength of those ridiculous looking legs when one of it, where the creature was coiled, came up horizontally sending the large serpent flying in the air. She shuddered as she saw it hit a swamp tree and go down into the water.

But it was not over yet. As they neared the shore, the serpent shot like a dart from the water right in front of the insect's head. Iora recoiled seeing its menacing yellow eyes and open mouth, with a dancing three-forked tongue. But this time the insect had had enough of fooling around. He caught the serpent's head in midair between the two semi-circular appendages on his mouth. He punctured the serpent's head and it writhed in pain. Iora shrieked all the while the rainbow serpent was held in his mouth. When the creature stopped squirming, Daddy Long Legs jerked his head and the serpent dropped limp in the water. It went down like a sinking rainbow.

Iora's legs shook when she descended on the shore. Owlus and Chinar, who had climbed up a tree seeing the second attack, came towards her. Owlus stared at the insect with a glint of respect, not giggling anymore, as he sat down clumsily. Soon the insect also brought Baba on the other side. The children surrounded him as soon as he landed.

"What was that?" asked Owlus.

"Why didn't it attack us on land? It could have done that," asked Iora.

"Yes, I think I saw it in the waters before," said Chinar.

"What do you think it was?" Baba asked back.

"Was it an agent of the anti-natural forces?" asked Iora, half hoping it was not true. They did not have such deadly attacks in mind.

Baba nodded. "It was the Rainbow Death Snake."

"But why didn't it attack us . . . or Iora when we were on land?" asked Chinar.

Baba didn't answer to his question. "Let's get going," he ordered.

"Because it wash afraid of Babash, afraid that he wash around," uttered Daddy Long Legs, his voice fizzed like the sound of wet sponge being squeezed. "It knew Babash couldn't swim properly, especially in a marshsh."

He had spoken for the first time. Chinar, Owlus and Iora had assumed he was dumb. They watched with interest as his mouth curved and moved behind the sharp semi-circular appendages.

He continued as they listened in complete silence, “Babash knew there wash danger lurking. So didn’t seek Pebbles’ help to crossh the bog.”

After a moment’s silence, Baba said, “I think we all should thank Daddy Long Legs and resume our journey. The light has reduced.”

The dark green light had darkened a few tones and assumed dusk grey shades.

All the three children thanked him politely and Baba patted his pulpy flat head, as it sat on the ground relaxing after the tussle.

“Hope to see you soon. Thank you again,” said Baba as Daddy Long Legs made a squashing sound in reply.

“I knew better than to trust serpents and their followers like Ghosts of Yellow Leaves,” said Owlus.

“Do not generalise, Owlus. The agent of Evil may be a snake, a beautiful bird, an attractive frog, a Twitter, a Pebble or an Amazon. You should learn to make the difference between ugly and evil,” said Baba.

The night was spent peacefully with all the three sleeping tight and Baba on the guard, resting only at intervals.

22
A Leap of Faith

"Today promises to be an interesting day. So gear up and keep your spirits high," said Baba the next morning.

"I hope it is not as interesting as yesterday," said Owlus, who looked less sulky.

The next day they started on their journey with the rising sun. They begun climbing the high mountain, happily leaving the swamp in the valley far behind. But this mountain was enormous. Its top was hidden in clouds. Waterfalls that plunged through narrow gorges seemed to be falling straight from the heavens.

"We have to reach the peak before noon," said Baba, who had climbed at the top of the canopy to have a better look.

"You mean before day after tomorrow noon, right?" said Owlus, looking at the overlapping crowns of foliage disappearing behind the clouds near the summit.

Iora also looked sceptical but Chinar didn't bother. He was occupied with a pineapple plant growing as an aerial plant on a tree trunk. He was a botanist's son but he had always seen pineapple plants growing only on the ground.

"I believe there are Suckers around here," said Baba and climbed down.

"It seems he's talking about you," Iora told Owlus.

It was the blossoming season and the patter of falling fruit bits on the ground was intercepted by the grunt of a dwarf bush baby, or a sudden movement of a tapir, or scurrying of a potto mother with her baby on her back. A faint fragrance of fruits and flowers filled the air as they walked with Chinar humming a tune. The whole world was at peace.

"I am thirsty," said Chinar. "I always thought that rainforest is full of water. When I got lost I realised it is easier to get food than to get water. If I had not found my way back to the river, I would have died of thirst, as if I were in a desert."

Owlus looked blank hearing the word 'desert'.

"Yes, there is a world of sand, a world of ice and a world of water outside the world of green. Father has told me," said Iora.

"We all know that every bit of information that has been stuffed in your head has been told by your father. So don't say that after every two sentences," said Owlus.

Iora frowned but didn't say anything.

"I know now that some lianas hold fresh drinkable water in them," said Chinar, and went ahead to cut a hanging liana with a piece of sharp bark. Clear inviting liquid poured out of it and he bent down to drink. He felt a sudden thrust to see that Iora had pushed him on the ground.

"What?" he asked.

"This liquid is clear cool poison!"

Owlus came forward and cut a similar looking liana and filled a leaf cup with the liquid. "Now this is clear cool water," Owlus said, giving the cup to Chinar, "and they say I go looking for trouble!"

Baba halted before a tree that had four huge roots evenly spaced out. They ran parallel to the ground instead of going down due to the thin rainforest soil.

"A truck can be parked between each of these!" said Chinar.

"Truck . . . never mind. I don't want to hear your stories," said Owlus.

Baba went around the tree knocking on its wide trunk.

"What's going on?" asked Owlus but Baba didn't answer.

When Baba knocked on a particular point, the buttress rose in the air with mud and pebbles falling down from its bottom, opening a gaping entrance to the tree trunk.

"You will go inside one by one. Just let loose your

body. If you don't try to touch or hold anything in the way, you'll be fine," said Baba.

"What is this all about?" asked Iora.

"The mouth is open and we don't have time. I'll let you know when we get out," said Baba. "We all will enter immediately one after the other. Owlus, you go in first."

"I am always the first one for all experimental work!" grumbled Owlus. He hesitated for a moment before stepping into the gaping hole.

After Iora and Chinar, Baba plunged himself inside as the root closed behind him.

Three continuous shrieks echoed in the hollow darkness. Iora, as soon as she put her first step, had realised that there was no ground underneath and she'd stepped into a deep drop. It was a tunnel that sucked them below. After going down they started being sucked up at a fast speed. The tunnel was at places straight, at others zigzagged and at yet others curvy. Flashes of light lighted up the surroundings time and again and they caught glimpses of flying squirrels, vampire bats, tapirs and black and white mice. Their minds swirled as they were puffed out one by one at the crown of a tree right near the top of the mountain.

They fell down on a tuft of spongy palm leaves, which made a bowl formation. The hollow opening of the trunk closed soon after spitting them out and became so inconspicuous that they couldn't have suspected that there was a mouth nearby. Baba was up on his feet but it took the three some time to get up and balance themselves.

"Funny, no one told me I was going to be tossed like a palm salad," said Owlus.

Iora, who stood near Baba, looked around her. They were on the top of a two-hundred-feet tall tree, which was lanky with a small crown. Its top looked like a breathing green bun. They carefully stepped on the canopy of the adjoining giant mahogany, leisurely spreading its limbs and swells of foliage on the adjoining treetops.

They came down the airborne highways made by latticework of lianas.

"That was a 'sucker' I suppose. But what exactly was it?" asked Iora.

"I thought you'd have a fair idea after being sucked yourself," said Owlus.

"Most rainforest trees are hollow from inside. They are perpendicular airborne caves," said Baba, who helped Chinar climb down.

"I know these hollow tree trunks serve as hunting and hiding grounds for some animals. I got glimpses of them!" said Chinar.

"Suckers are found only in this part of the Wacky Wilderness," continued Baba. "They can be used for transportation. They are connected with roots and trunks of various trees and underground channels."

"But how do you know where they are going to take you?" asked Owlus.

“Shape of the roots. The one that we came from had round ones, which take you to the top. The sharp root suckers take you down to the valley,” said Baba.

“But what if we want to go somewhere in between the hill?” asked Chinar.

“Well . . . different root shapes, angles and thickness denote different suckers. It can’t be learnt in one sitting. Thanks to them we are on time.”

The trio followed Baba to the peak. On the top of the mountain, which was more or less flat, there were no trees in sight. Instead it was covered with twenty feet tall grass, which swayed with the wind.

“Wow!” Chinar whistled.

They walked in a line behind Baba. It was noon and the sunrays filtered through the grasses more than the forest canopy. Finally, they came out in a clearing.

Right in the middle summit there was a large spring. It looked like a water volcano. The clear water with sunlight reflecting on it looked like molten crystal. The stream buzzed with activity. Small islands protruded at places. Crabs with human heads, brightly coloured mermaids, large prawns with tangerine armours and fish tails, otters with human hands and long silvery whiskers, double-tailed sunflower-yellow water serpents and shellfishes with braids of human hair swam, dived and dipped in the stream. Some creatures sunbathed on little islands and others merrily played on the bank.

They all looked at the intruders with polite curiosity, as Iora, Owlus and Chinar gawked at them. Baba stood with his hands resolutely on the ground. An algae green crab, twice the size of Baba, with a wig of reeds and a pair of thick moustaches came tottering towards them. His hard, burnished shell and claws looked strong enough to grip any one of them and turn him or her into minced meat.

"Are you Baba?" he asked.

"Yes. I believe you are Crabster," said Baba.

Crabster nodded, brought both his claws together, and put them on the ground. Baba also brought both the knuckles of his hands together and placed them on the ground. The songs and games had stopped and except the gurgling of water, there was no sound.

"I and the three little ones are here to meet the Aqua Angel," said Baba.

Everyone looked at the three startled children. A couple of jewel-eyed toads came hopping towards them and surveyed them closely.

"You have very less time in hand, my friend," said Crabster.

"I realise that," said Baba.

"The spring water is more tart than usual. The anti-natural forces are at large," said Crabster.

"I had guessed as much. Would appreciate if you could let me know where the Aqua Angel is today," said Baba.

"Just at the end of this peak, a few paces away," said Crabster.

Baba thanked him and started walking alongside the stream with the three amused children behind.

"By the way, I would have loved to spend time with you over some seaweed broth and discuss the forest affairs. It is not very often I get this chance. I hope we catch up under less demanding circumstances next time," said Crabster from behind.

Baba turned and said, "I feel likewise, Crabster. I earnestly hope there is a next time."

After walking a few paces alongside the stream, they reached the end of the peak where it fell down in a plunge. They could see other far-flung forested peaks but there was no bottom of this roaring fall visible. Thick mist shrouded the base.

"Now what? How do we go down?" asked Iora.

"Is there another shortcut like Sucker?" asked Chinar.

"The only shortcut is faith," said Baba.

"I hope it is not another whirling, sucking, tunnel-faced object," said Owlus.

"No, it is supposed to be quite stable, strong and yes, without a face or form."

"Invisible . . . huh? How will it transport us?" asked Iora.

"Like it has transported many before us."

Baba went right to the edge of the stream from where

it fell down the mountain and beckoned them to come. They approached cautiously on the slippery ground.

“Now hold my hand, all of you,” said Baba.

They placed their hands in Baba’s extended hand.

“Do you believe when I say that the Aqua Angel is at the bottom of this waterfall?”

“What’s there not to believe in?” said Owlus.

“Yes, I believe you,” said Iora. Chinar also nodded enthusiastically.

“This invisible transporting object called faith is going to take us down. Are you ready?” asked Baba.

Chinar was open to all unexpected things now. He looked at Baba and nodded in anticipation.

“Yes,” said Iora.

“Yeah, as long as I’m not to go in first,” said Owlus.

Baba held their hands, took a deep breath and leapt, taking them down the fathomless waterfall.

23
Yaya and Chirkut

They plummeted down and their screams drowned in the roaring water. They hadn't expected anything so drastic from Baba. Their speed reduced in the free fall and the stream falling with them converted into mist. All four of them crossed the mist hanging above the ground and landed gently on a water body. There was a dim blue fluorescent light all around. They didn't sink in the water; rather they stood on it, as if it was a supple piece of land. They looked above to see a hazy sight of the falling waterfall constantly vanishing midway in the air, just above the mist. The water below them flickered as if a thousand raindrops were falling on it, though there was no rainfall. This water body was the centre of the stream that flowed on both the sides of the jungle. The water in both the streams flowed either ways – coming towards the centre and going away from it.

On one corner, a thin tapering rock overhung horizontally just over the water body. Water droplets fell from this rock into the water body in a melodious rhythm. The drops originated from the rock itself. Droplets stopped falling as the four of them looked at the rock. They turned to observe the other surroundings when the droplets again started falling into the water body, playing the tune of a familiar song. Owlus and Iora looked at each other in wonder – it was a Twitterland folk song!

Oblivious of this fact, Chinar said, "Our fall was so thrilling! And now look at this magical water!"

He jumped and tried to sink in it but only managed to wet his feet.

"Some thrilling fall! My who-whole life came before my eyes . . . You suffer from this terrible habit of not keeping us informed about what is coming!" said Owlus to Baba.

He had not recovered from the shock of the fall. Iora lifted a handful of water in the cup of her palms to see that it still quivered like the water below.

"Where is the Aqua Angel, Baba?" asked Iora.

Baba broke the silence, but it was not Iora he addressed, "Please grace us with your divine presence, Aqua Angel."

"I am all around you, child," resonated a watery voice.

Some water rose from the shimmering water body in the fluorescent blue light and mingled with the overhanging mist. A shape formed in the air – of a lady with long flowing hair. The lower part of the form extended to the water body and remained connected with it. The dazzling beauty of the Aqua Angel made Iora think that she was the most gorgeous of all the Angels. They all bowed to her in admiration. Even Chinar had understood how to conduct himself in front of an Angel. Owlus seemed lost for words in her presence.

"So child, our dear forest faces another sinister blur. Do not worry, Iora, I will be there with you on the moonless night."

"You are so lovely . . ." said Iora, spellbound by her beauty.

The Aqua Angel smiled, lighting up the surroundings, making florescent blue light glow brighter.

"So are you, my child," she said in her restful, watery voice. "Where do you want me to come?"

"My Angel, it would be the Scar-faced River near Twitterland." Chinar volunteered this time.

Owlus and Iora looked at him; even Baba couldn't resist a smile.

"I will be there, children. Baba, my child, I bless you . . . May all of you be blessed by the benign Nature always," she said.

Her form dissolved in the blue light and the water hanging in the air fell down in a splash. Baba stood nearest to her and he was drenched to his last hair in divine water.

“Wow!” said Owlus.

“Double wow! I can be the follower of this Angel all my life!” added Chinar.

“If only I could have seen her for longer. I am sure my mother was like her,” said Iora.

“It seems Baba’s hearing problem is cured nowadays. Hope he heard the Angel calling him ‘child’. One overgrown child we have!” Owlus laughed heartily.

“If you all are done, we’ll proceed. Half the day still remains and we may be able to cover a good distance,” said Baba, moving towards the land from the water.

Chinar turned abruptly towards the musical droplets and stopped. Now the droplets played a tune of his favourite song from back home.

“This song is . . .” he started, but saw that the others had moved quite ahead. “Wait for me!” he shouted, and increased his pace to join them. “Those droplets there were playing my favourite song!” he panted when he was with them.

They all turned around to see it but there was nothing there. No trace of any water body, waterfall or stream. The usual thick mass of vines hanging from the top of the trees stood in the place of the water body.

By evening they had covered a considerable distance. Only Chinar stopped to observe aerial plants and epiphytes with rosettes of leaves overlapping each other. Some of these formed big bowls that served as aerial tanks in which tree frogs were housed. Baba led the children from one tree to another on lianas, which formed bridges between trees. Though the lianas shook dreadfully, they were strong enough to bear their weight. Baba seemed resolute on crossing another valley before nightfall, which they couldn't as it started raining. After a soggy dinner, Baba cleared a large hole in the middle of a tree and made it waterproof by putting a curtain of leaves at its mouth.

"You didn't tell me what the Aqua Angel does, Baba," said Chinar, whose cascade of questions had not stopped, in spite of being exhausted.

"Well, the Aqua Angel distributes and controls the water of the forest. She also has the Nature's healing powers. Rest later, Chinar. Right now, go to sleep."

Baba placed himself outside the crevice on the branch and dozed off after the children were asleep.

In the middle of the night, Iora woke up to a whooshing sound. She looked around. There was a torch of slow burning twigs on a side of the hole, placed by Baba. Owlus slept in a corner and the subdued snoring of Chinar was audible from the other corner. The rain had stopped and some raindrops trapped in branches still made a patting sound as they fell.

She lifted the transparent curtain to ask Baba if he'd heard something. There was complete darkness outside and it took her eyes some time to get acclimatised. She looked around but no outline of a hunched ape could be seen.

“Baba,” she whispered. No answer. “Baba,” she said, a little loudly this time.

Still no sound except the rustling of leaves. These were the night hours when the jungle activity came to a standstill. Not even the night animals were on prowl. The overwhelming stillness felt creepy. Iora turned to go inside and wake up the other two when a crack shattered the calm of the night behind her.

“What is the hurry, my dear,” came a guttural voice.

Iora halted and turned around slowly not knowing what to expect. A whiff of putrid smell filled her nostrils.

A gargantuan half-bird half-lizard, whose head reached the high branch on which Iora stood, rested its jagged beak on the other end of the branch. Looking at the outline of its head, Iora wondered how big its neck and body would be. There was a steady droning sound but she couldn’t make out what it was.

“What’s happening?” asked Owlus, as he came out with the torch.

The torch lit up the branch. The bird lifted its head and they saw its long neck. Its whole body was decomposed and putrid smell emanated from it. It was pale and bore the whiteness of a lizard’s belly. Claws at the back of its neck ran down its spine. A bright pink cravat made out of silkworm threads was tied tightly around its pulpy neck and a night smelling orchid was thrust on the top of its pus-filled skull. A swarm of hornets hovered above its head. It raised its beak, pierced a giant hornet with its teeth and gulped it. In spite of this, the rest of the hornets kept hovering near it in a stupor.

Its eyes did not glow in the light of the torch, as other living animals, and Iora and Owlus saw maggots crawling and feeding on its neck. Perhaps its long beak had seen better days. The bird was the wretched remains of some long gone creature.

"You look positively ill . . . rather . . . dead!" said Owlus.

Chinar also came out rubbing his eyes. He rubbed his eyes again on seeing the bird.

The creature didn't look too happy with Owlus's question and answered back gratingly, "I am the most beautiful, charming and graceful bird in the whole jungle! I don't blow my own trumpet, else I'd have said that I am the most eligible for Bird of the Jungle contest. Anyway, I don't care about the opinion of a bunch of fledglings! How right was Cooka . . . Oops!"

"I want to know right now who this Cooka is!" shouted Iora.

What . . . what do you want?" asked Owlus, who had got knots of repulsion in his stomach.

"We want your blood, Iora," came another voice from a branch below.

A thuggish-looking dwarf forest ogre climbed up the branch near the bird's head. There was a hole in place of one of his eyes but his intact eye glinted maliciously at them. He had a savage mouth and humped shoulders.

He took one step and jerked as if he was about to lose balance. But he took another step and jerked again. Iora realised he had a limp.

"Don't worry; you'll die next to your dear Baba. The good always die young, they say. That's why I say be bad and live long!"

"Is Baba with you?" asked Chinar, losing all hope of being rescued this time.

"Where is Baba? What have you done to him?" cried Iora.

"Oh, you would like to see? Very well," said the dwarf ogre and made an ominous call.

Leaves below them rustled and they saw something being raised in air. It seemed it was a huge snake raising its hood. But it wasn't a snake. It soon came in their circle of light and they saw a broad flat ribbon vine, which usually spreads for long distances on the jungle floor. It stood upright in the air with something entangled spirally at its upper end. They got a glimpse of rusty brown hair through the tight fisted grip of the vine. Baba was wrapped inside it!

"Set him free at once, you weirdoes!" cried Owlus.

The ogre let out a derisive laugh. The bird's head, which would have fallen apart on touch, advanced and said, "My dear kids, didn't your parents teach you to respect elders? I am 794 years old. Don't go on my youthful looks."

She gestured to the ogre who then made the ominous

call again. More ribbon vines rose around them, their ends bent like an attacking snake.

"This is for your own good," said the bird.

The ogre made another eerie sound and the vines attacked Iora, Owlus and Chinar from all sides.

24
An Unusual Garden

The three of them found themselves floating in air in the rib-breaking grip. The flat flaps had shut their face. They could not see or speak and all the swaying made them giddy. Iora was too suffocated to think or even feel the fear of what lay ahead.

After what seemed like a long time, the numbing grip on Iora loosened and she gasped for a mouthful of air. The ribbon vine had dropped its grip around her and lay limp on the ground. She was in a small clearing in the forest and the night sky was visible above her head. Seeing the position of constellations, she realised the night was in its last hours. The moon was a thin crescent, indicating that there were not many nights left before the moonless night. The visibility here was clearer as there was no forest canopy overhead. After a few moments when her eyes adjusted to the light, the obscure outlines started taking shapes.

Some large plants grew at a little distance from each other. Three ribbon vines at the other end of the clearing stood still in the air with three bundles. Baba, Owlus and Chinar had not been released. She began to go towards them when her surroundings lighted up. She turned around to see the rotting bird and the dwarf ogre coming towards her from the woods. The ogre carried the torch dropped by Owlus. In that light she could see the entire front of the bird. She had long talons, a muscular body and a long neck with the head precariously perched on it. However, flesh was absent from many parts of her body and even as she walked, decomposing bits fell on the ground. The orchid placed on her putrid head was one of the most repulsive sights Iora had ever seen. Its sweet smell mixed with the smell of rot was enough to set one's intestines in turmoil. The claws on her wings and at the back of her neck running down her spine were clearly visible now. Hornets still hovered over her head and she lifted her beak now and then to catch and gulp down one.

Iora could run away but she stood firmly because Baba, Owlus and Chinar were still trapped.

Before either of the two could speak, Iora said, "So, what next?"

"Well, though I like you, we've to get rid of you first. Show her my garden, Chirkut," said the reptilian bird.

"Yes, our Garbage Disposal Unit is waiting eagerly," said Chirkut, raising his torch.

Iora looked around. Other than some huge plants, there was nothing. These plants looked spectacular.

"I've always believed in freedom of choice," said the bird, clattering her heavy beak, which was hardly in control of itself because of the rotting skin.

"See what Lady Yaya the Spirit is saying? You are lucky. How do you want to die?"

Iora said nothing.

"I will give you some choices. Three units out here have been particularly requested as they deliver good quality work. I'll present them to you and then you can decide."

Iora's mind had been working hard to find a way to set Baba, Owlus and Chinar free. But she couldn't think of any way to overcome three hefty ribbon vines, the ogre and the bird simultaneously. The ogre, meanwhile, went near a beautiful cactus. It had a large, curved white and orange candle leaf in the centre, between rosettes of outer leaves.

"This one here is Candleflory. You will be placed in the middle and the candle will squirt a liquid on you. It will then twine around you and before you know you'll be dead and gone."

The cactus looked beautiful and Iora eyed it in disbelief.

He went to another plant and lighted the area with his torch.

"Sundew is her name. Isn't she beautiful?"

With thick bottle green leaves and a large bright

yellow flower in the centre, this plant was indeed breathtaking. The flower had sticky, bright tentacles with blue rounded ends.

"You are glued when you are placed on the flower. Her tentacles stick to your skin and burst into the nerves, sucking your blood at leisure. You may die a slow painful death."

"And this last one," said Chirkut, beaming at another plant, "is the favourite amongst all. He is the Old Coaster. Though not beautiful, he is the most experienced and can digest anything. And, mind you, he does not give a painful death. He paralyses you and you die a slow painless death while the plant and other meat-eating ants do their job."

This last plant was a lump of vegetation with no flower but small hooked tentacles all over. Iora tried to work out some kind of a plan.

"We do not have forever, girl. Lady Yaya the Spirit has been kind enough to give you the best of options. You see the other plants? They are well equipped with thrusting and cutting weapons!"

"Chirkut, we have to finish this task before dawn. And we wouldn't be giving the other three these choices. Wouldn't it be fun to put the fat ape in Muttercutter? And that odd, foreign-looking kid should be thrown . . ."

Iora had had enough. She took three somersaults, got to the bird and thrust her feet forcefully on her chest. But to her disgust, her feet sank inside the bird's decomposing belly and she fell down with the rot covering her legs. Yaya powerfully stood on her place and Chirkut looked rather bored.

"Good try. But not good enough. You should be with the Amazons."

"Let's finish it, Lady, we do not have time."

Chirkut looked at the sky, which neared the crack of dawn.

"Yeah, I have to get my beauty sleep," said Yaya tiredly.

Chirkut made the same sound and the limp ribbon vine got Iora in its grasp. It rose above Sundew and dropped her right onto it. Iora didn't even get time to shout as she saw herself nearing the expectantly moving yellow tentacles.

Iora shut her eyes as she fell. She landed on something leafy and opened her eyes expecting tentacles closing on her. To her relief she found herself lying on a broken branch under which the tentacles of Sundew fumbled to get to her. She quickly jumped away from the man-eating plant. She was surprised to see a fifteen-foot tall, hairy ape-man who had pinned the ogre beneath his feet and held the bird by her disintegrating neck. The hornets continued to hover over the choking bird's head. She could see the ape-man's back and head covered with wiry hair. On the other side there was a strange-looking woman making the same sound that was made by the ogre to control the ribbon vines. In no time the ribbon vines had placed Baba, Owlus and Chinar to the ground and fallen limply around them. Gulping and gasping for air, the three of them looked around.

Owlus and Chinar stood clueless, not knowing whether to run or stand. Baba took account of the situation in a jiffy and rushed towards the struggling ogre and bird. The choking sounds coming from the bird's squeezed throat and the ogre's yelps sounded pathetic. Iora felt like requesting the giant to release them. The woman followed Baba. Iora saw her in the light of the torch, which had been dropped by the ogre near the ape-man's feet. She was short and slightly built with a deformed face, short and stiff hair and a light moustache. But there was something strangely familiar in her pallid eyes. Iora wondered but didn't say anything. Baba looked at the back of the ape-man and went around him, avoiding the falling rotten pieces. Iora, still shuddering, followed him.

The ape-man smiled at Baba with ease, exposing a set of yellow teeth with prominent canines set in a broad mouth.

Baba turned to the woman. "Are you . . ."

The woman gave a knowing smile. "It took me some time to wake *Homo-gigantis* and to convince him to come. I had to promise him a month's supply of slugs, black flies and Fermenting Fungus. There was no other way. *Homo-gigantis* are the only ones who can counter these two dark spirits," she said.

Her voice was loud and husky and sounded huskier as she shouted above the din. She held Baba's hand and took him to a side.

"You must hurry. I'll take care of this."

"Thanks a lot," said Baba. He took Iora's hand, leading her through the flesh eating plants moving their appendages hungrily.

Owlus and Chinar stood on the other end of the clearing. They hurried after Baba without looking back at the violence behind.

The rumbling voice of *Homo-gigantis* cut through the shouts, "Don't worry, lady. I will take these two to my grandma. She washes such sinful souls in boiling water."

When they were considerably away, Baba stopped and asked, "Are you all right?"

"Oh yes, I just had the best time of my life," said Owlus.

"Yeah, I guess I am fine," said Chinar, examining himself.

"I am quite okay, Baba. It was so very close! But how are you and who was the woman who came to save us?" asked Iora.

"We've to clear this valley before dawn," said Baba, swinging to another branch.

***

Baba stopped a little after dawn as the morning contingents of animals went about their duties.

"For the time being we're out of the danger zone. Mind you, only for the time being. You all must take some rest," said Baba, looking at the exhausted children.

He arranged a place with soft leaves out of the way of the passing animals.

"Take a nap," he told them after they'd eaten grapefruits and red ants' headless bodies, which Chinar squinted while eating.

But Baba insisted he eat that to give him energy.

"Aren't you going to sleep?" Iora asked Baba who looked ill.

"I'll be fine," he said, sitting on guard on the branch as the three of them made themselves comfortable.

Iora looked at Baba with concern but knew it would be in vain to force him. She tried to sleep but sleep didn't come to her. Yaya had said 'Cooka' and stopped. Was it indeed Cockatoo who had helped *Homo-diabolus* seventy years back? Why didn't he believe her when she told him what she'd heard near the well? Who else could come near their well at that late hour? Why did he want her father Heron to fetch him jaguar skin and why didn't he stop him when Heron suggested getting Black Piranha teeth when it could be life threatening? She didn't want to voice her thoughts to anyone else or place her grandfather under anyone else's suspicion. It took her all her will to not suspect her own grandfather without proof. She went off to sleep with a heavy head.

By the time they got up it was noon, time for the jungle's afternoon siesta. Baba sat alertly but looked much more haggard and gaunt. His eyes had swollen and it looked as if the muscles of his mouth pained as he smiled. Even Owlus and Chinar noticed it much more clearly.

"Are you hurt, Baba?" asked Owlus.

"Fine as always," said Baba, still smiling. "Yaya and Chirkut have unwittingly brought us closer to our destination. By day after tomorrow evening we should reach the Tree Angel."

"But I really think you need some sleep, Baba," said Chinar.

When he didn't reply, Owlus asked, "Who were those two characters, Baba?"

"The strongest of the dark spirits lives below the jungle and protects *Homo-diabolus*. But this sub-bird, Yaya the Spirit, is also a very strong underworld dark spirit. The ogre is Chirkut, Yaya's pet. This bird once walked the earth in ancient times, alive and righteous. Non-jungle dwellers exterminated her when they raided our jungles. Later, she was invoked from the dead by *Homo-diabolus* and given unnatural powers. She fed on the corpses and dragged even the good spirits to the underworld. But she was put to rest when the Five Angels met last, seventy years ago. I've come across many lesser evil spirits walking the jungle in the last few days. But the fact that Yaya has risen from the dead indicates that the anti-natural forces are gaining power."

Iora, Owlus and Chinar looked at each other perturbed.

"But you wouldn't tell us who that ugly woman was who saved us?" asked Owlus.

"Come children, this is the last Angel we've to meet and then you can head home to Twitterland. After the moonless night, when this is all over, we can go look for Chinar's folks," said Baba.

The word 'home' made the three of them silent as they followed Baba. They even forgot they had to find the Spirit of the Jungle. Chinar felt homesick remembering his mother.

"You should taste the *kheer* and jelly cream that Ma makes . . ."

Owlus also had a strong urge to hug his father and mother and even his sister, Fowlus. The thoughts of her father and grandfather had been occupying Iora's mind, though she tried not to talk about it. It seemed like forever since she'd left Twitterland. Will I ever go back home, each of them thought as they silently followed Baba.

25
The Three Friends

"Watch out!" cried Chinar. It was late afternoon; two days since they had been walking downhill. A large, black gorilla charged at Iora as they passed his territory. Baba gestured them to stand still. Chinar had a strong urge to turn on his heels and run. He clutched Baba's hand, who stood nonchalantly. They saw other gorillas scattered here and there and some baby gorillas playing, not minding the intruders. The large gorilla advancing towards them came very near and displayed its menacing teeth. After this short display, he stopped a little distance away. Since they did not move, he quietly turned and went back to his troupe.

Owlus and Iora were trained and didn't think of this incidence twice but Chinar kept nudging them with questions.

"Oh boy, aren't you one overexcited non-jungly!" said Owlus.

"Gorillas are introverts, peaceful and level-headed apes and not rowdy like chimps. They may charge on you if you enter their territory but if you don't run, they retreat without harming," said Iora.

"You know I find them to be magnificent. But Father doesn't like them, as he doesn't like the jungles. He calls the rainforests 'Green Hell'. I do not agree with him though!"

"Can't understand why he keeps quoting his father if he doesn't agree with him!" fumed Owlus.

The sun had not yet gone down when they reached the valley. Baba continued walking in the narrow valley and didn't climb another hill. Owlus's homesickness had worn off. They had no time to think about it during the taxing journey in the daytime. Baba regularly gave them a lot of nourishing stuff to munch on and applied all sorts of herbs and snail secretions to cure their blistered feet and bruised limbs overnight. They were generally okay by the next morning but now the continuous fatigue caught up with them. No one complained except Owlus and that too not often. He observed Baba's bloated face and limbs and understood that Baba was so badly hurt that even his potent potions had stopped working on him.

More than his blisters, fatigue and homesickness, what was paramount on Owlus's mind was the Spirit of the Jungle. They had hardly any days left to the moonless night and there was no hope of finding it. If what he had heard was true, he, along with Iora, would die on the moonless night if it was not found, even if the jungle was saved. How unfair! Owlus kept thinking to himself.

In his desperation, he started asking birds, insects, animals, trees, anything that came in his way, "Are you the Spirit of the Jungle?"

Though Iora got really irritated by this behaviour of Owlus, his anxiety rubbed off on her as well.

"Tell me, Baba, will we find the Spirit of the Jungle?" she asked yet again.

"I am sure you can find her, Iora," answered Baba.

'You can find her?' Does that mean no one else is going to help me out in this? Not even Baba? thought Iora, feeling let down.

They were advancing in the valley when all of a sudden the ground began to roll from side to side and up and down. Chinar felt as if he was riding a turbulent sea.

Baba shrieked, "Move back! Move back!"

They all fell on the ground and slithered their way back. As soon as they moved back the ground stopped shaking.

"What was that?" said Iora, horrified.

"It was a brief earthquake, what else?" said Chinar.

As soon as Owlus moved a step or two ahead the ground started to shake again.

"What on jungle is this?" he fumed, moving back before he fell down.

Baba was about to answer when the ground shivered again, though not so badly this time.

A crack appeared a little ahead of them and a cluster of burly roots emerged from it and rose high above. They stood twisted and curled and the thickness of each of them was similar to a middle-sized tree trunk. All the roots with pointed ends stood swaying and twitching as if they were made of muscles.

"Let's go from the other side," said Owlus, scared at the sight.

He had had enough with the ribbon vines and these roots looked much more menacing and sturdy.

"We are here to meet the Tree Angel," said Baba to the roots instead.

In the dim light of the evening, they could see two hollow wooden eyes opening in each root. The eyes were black holes and wooded eyelashes blinked on them, making a snapping sound.

A root from the midst of the cluster opened its mouth and peeked out of the swaying huddle. "Are you *the three friends*?" It asked in a voice which made them remember a saw moving on wood.

"Yes, we are," answered Iora.

"Then you can pass through. But before that, come and put your hand in my mouth to prove it," said the middle root in its abrasive voice.

"And who would you be?" asked Owlus, scared but nevertheless his usual unrestrained self.

"We are the guards of the Tree Angel," said the root, unblinking.

"Why does the Tree Angel need guards? Can't it protect itself?" persisted Owlus.

All the hollow eyes of the roots turned on Owlus and opened their mouths wide open as if in surprise. But Owlus realised it was not in surprise. Sharp wooden spikes came out of all the mouths except the mouth of the middle root, which had opened as big as a small cave in a silent scream.

Owlus was scared but because all the three – Baba, Iora and Chinar – looked at him disapprovingly, he went on in defiance, "Look at these goons trying to scare me for a standard query! I'll find some other way to get to the Angel!"

"Stop it, Owlus!" warned Baba.

But Owlus tried to go ahead, avoiding the cluster of angry roots. A root went swishing down in the ground from the huddle and re-emerged in front of Owlus blocking his way. It started to attack him like a wild serpent with a thrusting spike for a mouth.

"Stop, please!" shouted Baba, and the root stopped in midair.

"We are the three friends," said Baba pointing at Iora, Owlus and himself. "We are ready to put our hands in your mouth," and he moved towards the middle root.

"All three together!" screeched the middle root.

Iora went towards it. Owlus frowned at the root, which had come to attack him, before he joined Iora and Baba who stood waiting for him.

"Iora and I; friends! Ha!"

The middle root bent down to their level and its mouth opened just enough to let the three hands in. Baba, Iora and Owlus held their hands together and inserted them inside the root's hollow mouth. Iora's hand scratched against its rough inner walls but she didn't blink. Chinar stood at a distance, looking at it with interest.

As soon as they put their hands inside, Owlus half expecting his hand to be bitten off, the root spat them out and they fell on the ground. Baba managed to get his bulky self up swiftly and Iora and Owlus got up with their 'Ahs' and 'Ouches'.

"What's wrong with you!" cried Owlus, taking his hair off his eyes.

The root twitched its dark void of a mouth as if it had tasted something unsavoury.

"Animals . . . this is the first and last time you've tested my nerves! I do not want two friends and one protector. I want three friends! Leave aside meeting the Angel, if I don't get the third friend right now, you can forget about going back with your limbs intact!" Its voice became more and more jarring.

"What shall we do now, Baba, we're stuck . . ." said

Iora. Owlus didn't say anything; he looked at the roots anxiously.

Baba rubbed his hand on his receding forehead.

He was lost in thought when Chinar came forward and said, "I am the third friend."

Baba looked at him in alarm. "But, Chinar, do you know what you're getting into? You will become a part of this mission and the dark forces will turn against you!" he said.

"Not forgetting that you might, you know . . . die as we've still not found the Spirit of the Jungle," said Iora.

Owlus nodded gravely and added, "By the way, does anyone know if a non-jungle dweller can pose as our friend? I hope these big . . . roots . . . do not rearrange our limbs . . ."

The ground shivered and roots from the cluster went inside and re-emerged on all the sides forming a solid cage around the foursome; the empty eyes fixed and the spikes aimed at them. One wrong move and Baba knew they would be done for good.

"I am ready," said Chinar, unflinching.

"Very well then," said the middle root and bent near them, opening its hollow mouth.

Iora, Chinar and Owlus held their hands together, looked in each other's eyes, and thrust their hands inside the open mouth.

The roots started giggling and released their hands gently. The spikes went swooshing inside the mouths of the respective roots. And the roots in turn forming the cage disappeared in the ground and re-appeared in a cluster near the middle root again.

"Go straight ahead across this path," said the middle root, pointing the way.

Wanting to get out of this place as soon as possible, they started quickly. But a root emerged from the ground in front of Baba and blocked his path.

"Only these three can go," it said in a voice that made it amply clear that there was no room for discussion.

Darkness had descended. Baba lit three torches for them.

"I will be waiting here," he said.

With torches in their hands the trio went ahead, not knowing what to expect. After a while they saw light emitting from behind some trees.

"I think we've reached the Angel," said Iora, not feeling confident without Baba.

She had heard descriptions of the Angels but it was mostly hearsay and no one claimed to have seen any of them firsthand. She had seen how different the Bird Angel was believed to be in Twitterland depictions. They went behind the trees from where the light filtered.

The place was lighted up with golden light and it seemed some plants were on fire. But on a closer look, Iora realised that it was not fire but light emitting from blonde hanging roots of the tall plants. There was a shallow pool of crystal clear water, in the middle of which stood a stout tree. It had olive green crown and its roots spreading sideways could be seen through the sparkling water till the point where they went inside the ground. A layer of mist hung around its trunk forming a halo. Small blue fireballs resembling tiny stars grew on the tree.

They slowly approached the tree and bowed. The air carried fragrance of various rainforest flowers and herbs and they felt completely rejuvenated breathing it in.

"Welcome to my humble abode, children," came a gentle voice.

They couldn't see a mouth or eyes on the Tree Angel but they saw some leaves rustling.

Some way to welcome! What's with those ugly roots? Owlus thought.

"My dear Owlus, those roots may get a little dramatic at times but they are affectionate beings and solid protection against the dark agents," came the voice with the breeze.

Owlus felt mortified about the Angel having read his thoughts. That was so eerie. He immediately tried to stop thinking before the Angel could read his thoughts again.

"My Angel, we are so honoured to meet you," said Iora, bowing again.

"It is my pleasure to meet such brave children," came the rustling reply.

Before Iora could say anything else, Owlus, not able to contain himself, said, "My Angel, where can we find the Spirit of the Jungle? We have only three more days to go."

"When one conquers, it is the consequence of not only action but also patience. So don't despair; desperation is the last path that can lead to your destination."

They felt as if someone had patted them on their heads. There was nothing but whispering breeze, perhaps sent by the moving leaves of the Angel.

"Wouldn't you invite me over, Iora?"

"Of course, my Angel. Please grace us with your presence on the banks of the Scar-faced River near Twitterland."

"So, we'll meet on the moonless night."

***

The trio came back with their torches hearing the chuckles of the roots from a distance. The roots looked kind of cute and seemed to be good pals with Baba now.

"It was totally unnecessary, it seems, to stop you from visiting the Tree Angel. But to think of, it is good we did, or else we would have missed your company."

"How do you impress people? I fail to understand," said Owlus when they were out of earshot but still in the vicinity of the roots. Baba had planned to spend the night there.

Iora told Baba all about the Angel and its abode. Chinar's train of questions blew a whistle at this.

"It is the Tree of Life," said Baba, "the Angel of Wisdom – wisdom with roots. Its roots spread beneath the soil of the forest, bind the earth and provide nourishment to the jungle. This Angel manages the earthquakes. It also releases air, which breathes life into all the living, controls the tempests and gales, and guides the clouds to the jungle sky."

"But doesn't Thunderbird control the rain?" asked Chinar.

"Well, this is the beauty of the jungle. The jungle elements work in synergy with each other. That is what brings stability. Rain by the Thunderbird, sunrays by the Insect Angel, balance and survival by the Animal Angel, water by the Aqua Angel and air by the Tree Angel, they all are immensely powerful yet interdependent on each other and make the jungle a whole and pulsating entity."

Baba was in a good mood and his inflamed face seemed better in his cheerfulness.

"This is a safe area and we can spend the night here . . . It is indeed a great achievement that you have met all the Angels!"

"It wouldn't have been possible without yours or Beetle's help. Hope he is fine now . . ." said Iora.

"Yes, we could have never done it alone," conceded Owlus.

"You never know, Owlus. Creatures don't undertake things fearing failure." He turned to Iora and said, "It takes a lot of courage to just get up and do it like you did."

Baba beamed at them.

"Perhaps your motivation has been the competitive streak in you, Owlus, but it takes courage to stand up to your decision and face it till the end."

"Are you saying all this to make me feel good before I die?" asked Owlus. "Did you understand any bit of what the Tree Angel said when I asked about the Spirit of the Jungle?" he said, turning to Iora.

Iora just shrugged.

"And of course, Chinar," continued Baba, not hearing their conversation, "you have an extraordinarily open mind and willingness to learn. You've displayed commendable morality when you offered yourself as the third friend, knowing you could've been safer otherwise . . . I am proud of you all!"

Chinar looked pleased and Iora also smiled.

"We have three challenging days ahead. I'll have to use all my skills to get you to Twitterland. We may part ways after that . . ." said Baba pausing for a while. "So tonight I'll fix up a little feast. I can leave you in the safe hands of the roots while I make the arrangements."

"I hope the 'hands of the roots' are safer than their mouths," said Owlus, glancing at the limp, dozing-off silhouette of the cluster at a distance.

"You don't look too good, Baba," said Iora.

But Baba did not listen. Within moments four vine hammocks were tied to the trees in a circle and a bonfire was lit in the middle. Baba went to make the arrangements for dinner and they climbed on their comfortable hammocks.

Baba returned in no time, his hands full of food. But he was not alone. A train of tiny jungle nymphs flew behind him, their backs twinkling. Chinar was fascinated to see them and Iora and Owlus also gazed at them, forgetting everything else. They'd heard about them in Twitterland stories but never seen one.

"I found my friends," said Baba, placing the raw food near the bonfire.

"Are these the nymph flies?"

Baba nodded. He said something to them in Nymphfli, which contained a lot of long 'iiiiiiis' and 'oooooos', as he started preparing the meal. The nymph flies went one by one to Iora, Owlus and Chinar and nodded their heads with two antennas so sweetly that it made even Owlus smile. Iora greeted them but the nymph flies didn't understand Jungly. They were all of different colours – pollen yellow, sky blue, sapphire green, reddish golden . . . After the thirty odd nymph flies had greeted them, they fluttered their transparent wings and made an orchid formation just above the bonfire. Iora wanted to offer help to Baba but she knew he wouldn't accept it.

The nymph flies began to sing a song in Nymphfli. It was very soothing and they listened to it spellbound. The flies had lighted a ring of fire in the air and jumped through it, doing midair somersaults, holding hands and making formations of trumpeting elephants, cascading waterfalls, otter feeding its little ones . . . They enacted a story through the song. Their fast moving bodies left trails of light, which faded gradually.

By the time they'd completed the second song, Baba had finished preparing dinner. Iora, Owlus and Chinar would have loved to see another act but they got down seeing the nymph flies gather near the bonfire. It had been a while since they had enjoyed so much. The nymph flies sat in a line on one side of the fire and Iora, Owlus and Chinar sat opposite them. Baba placed lotus leaves and told everyone to help themselves. Chinar was stunned at Baba's efficiency at preparing such a spread in no time. Fish eggs tossed in butter plant secretion, fruit salad containing seven jungle fruits, sweetened cracker leaf wafers, sour okapi milk in bee honey and not to forget the delectable palm salad. Owlus gorged as if there was no tomorrow. There was a heap of flowers with pale brown petals and bright yellow pollens placed in front of the nymph flies and they munched on them making, what seemed, sounds of satisfaction.

Baba had not forgotten the roots. Before he began eating he went to them carrying a pitcher of bark containing a red liquid. The roots had been indifferent to the nymph flies' performance. But at the sight of the pitcher they stood straight. The pitcher size looked less than a gulp for one of them. They bent down opening their mouths so that Baba could reach them. He tipped a few drops of the liquid in each mouth. It looked like a bird feeding its chicks. The only difference was that the chicks were the size of the bird and the bird was the size of the chicks. After swallowing the drink the roots thanked Baba so profusely that he blushed as he walked back.

***

The next day when they started early morning, Iora saw Baba's face and realised how unwell he was. He had looked better in the soft light of the bonfire. Nevertheless, he smiled. But in his attempt to smile, the stiffness of his inflated face got more evident and the effort he had to make to even blink his eyes made his state more obvious. He hardly spoke that morning and even his farewell to the roots was concise. Owlus and Chinar also realised this and followed him silently throughout the day. Baba took most unexpected shortcuts that were not exactly free of danger. The thoughts about Cockatoo throbbed relentlessly in Iora's mind as they headed towards Twitterland.

The following day they crossed the valley much before noon and were halfway up a hill when Baba turned to them and said, "Follow me close behind in a line. This area has Fiend's Mouths. They are deep water-filled holes and in each hole an aquatic creature resides. If you slip in it there is no chance of coming out as these creatures pull you down in a whirlpool. Do as I say! Avoid the Curtain Fig Trees like black fever, even if you've to step on a scorpion. The vines climbing their hanging roots have poison-filled thrones."

They walked vigilantly behind Baba in a line. They saw many Curtain Fig Trees with their clusters of hanging roots covered with bright green poison vines. There were some holes, which they would have mistaken for guiltless little ponds, had they not known better.

They were about to cross the area of the Curtain Fig Trees and Fiend's Mouths when there came a familiar voice, accompanied by a pungent smell, "What's the hurry, my dears?"

They were ahead in a straight line with Baba in the lead and Iora at the end. Iora had a nauseating feeling as she turned to face Yaya and Chirkut standing behind them. A swarm of dazed hornets hovered over Yaya's head and Chirkut stood conceitedly at her feet.

"Did you think your disproportioned friends could stop a well-proportioned bird like me? Wishful thinking, my dears, wishful thinking!"

"We don't have time, my lady. We should capture Iora and then deal with the others."

"Yeah, that's right," said Yaya, who just had to bring her beak down to hit Iora or thrust her talon to knock the life out of her.

Without a moment's delay, Yaya bent her rotting head backwards to swing it ahead with full force at Iora. In a flash, Baba swung on a hanging liana towards Yaya and Chirkut. He let go of the liana as he approached them, caught hold of one of the bird's talons and Chirkut's hand as he landed. With a surge of manic energy, he pushed both of them along with himself in a nearby Fiend's Mouth. For a fraction of a second Iora, Chinar and Owlus saw a long lizard's neck emerge from the hole. A standing line of yellow hair made a crest all along its spine. It coiled around all three of them and dragged them down in the blink of an eye.

Two screeches could be heard going down. They got fainter and fainter and finally faded into nothingness.

Iora stood shell-shocked, frozen in her place. Owlus stood with both his hands on his ears, as if blocking the sound would make things better. It was only the sobs of Chinar that stirred the ensuing silence and brought Iora and Owlus back to their senses.

"No . . . no . . . no . . ." Iora mumbled, shaking her head from side to side.

Owlus lost balance and slipped to the ground, his hands still on his ears. Iora felt hot all over, a rush of blood making her red in the face. Tears welled in her eyes as she walked in a trance towards the Curtain Fig Tree, adjoining the pond. She went at the edge of the pond and shouted at the top of her voice, "Baba!"

Her voice bumped across the walls of the hole and came back to her in a mocking echo. She kept shouting till the time Owlus and Chinar approached and pulled her away from the Fiend's Mouth. Now it was their turn to call out for him but their tearful calls went unheeded and the pool sat there glistening at them, unstirred.

26
The Dying Forest

They sat near the deadly pool for long. Finally, Owlus got up and extended a hand to Iora and Chinar. Their sobs had died away and a feeling of dismay had come over them. They walked silently, away from the Fiend's Mouth – or was it Baba's grave? The thought was unbearable. It didn't take them long to reach the peak. Iora kept turning back, hoping to see Baba come behind them.

"This is just a nightmare. I'll soon wake up," Owlus repeated to himself.

After reaching the peak they sat down under a tree. Was it their state of mind or was everything around them wilting? Was it cloudy or the night sky had actually become lightless, barren of all the stars and constellations? A rock was placed on their hearts and they could no longer walk with its weight. The shared grief grafted a bond between them like nothing else could have. Iora lit a small fire.

"I wish Yaya had killed me instead of Baba. I lost my mother before I could even know her and I may lose my father tomorrow. Yaya should have taken me. Oh poor, poor Baba . . ." said Iora.

Owlus put an arm around her and Chinar patted on her hand. They sat huddled, gazing into the fire as their last hope turned to ashes.

***

Iora was cornered. Yaya with her putrid talons advanced from one side and an ugly crocodile from the other.

How did Yaya survive the Fiend's Mouth? If Yaya could, then Baba must have made it too! wondered Iora, in spite of the danger on all sides.

She moved back and felt pebbles slip under her feet. She turned around to see herself a step away from a deep chasm, at the bottom of which giant leeches had opened their slimy tubular mouths expectantly. As she turned to find some route of escape, a familiar rusty figure came behind Yaya.

She cried in delight, "Baba!"

Baba jumped forward to reach her but she lost balance and slipped down the abyss, her cries bouncing on the lifeless walls.

Iora jerked out of sleep, sweating. It was late morning and she saw Owlus stirring from his sleep. They both sat up and looked at each other trying to recall what had ensued the previous evening.

They woke up Chinar, who mumbled, "I'll be up in five minutes, Baba . . ."

He opened his eyes to see the drawn faces of Iora and Owlus. It all came back to him instantly.

They had not eaten anything since the day before and their stomachs growled. Owlus and Iora looked around but they'd never seen the jungle so bleak. Trees stood sagging and withered, as if someone had sucked the life out of them. The usual morning traffic of animals was non-existent and not a single creature was in sight. A creepy immobility had overcome the jungle.

"What's wrong?" Owlus heard himself asking through the deathly quiet.

"Let's climb to the canopy and find out."

"Would you want to come along?" Owlus asked a dazed Chinar.

"Yes . . . Yes please take me along . . ."

They helped Chinar up the wilting tree. It was a difficult climb as the lianas had dried up and snapped when they leaned for support. Even the bark of the tree trunk and small branches broke as they climbed, making it very precarious. Iora was the most proficient in climbing and led the way. It took them a while to reach the dried up crown of the tree. Their hearts sank at the sight from the treetop. It was not only this patch that was dying, it was the entire forest; all the hills beyond. They were on the canopy on the hilltop and could see a considerable distance on all the sides. Brownish-green blotches where the vegetation had died on various hills spread, as they saw, like disfiguring fungus.

"What do we do? We do not even know which direction to take. If only Baba were here . . ." sighed Owlus.

"Tonight is the moonless night. We may not be able to reach Twitterland, but we must try," said Iora.

"Baba said he would have to utilise the best of his skills to get us back on time. We are directionless and we don't stand a chance," said Chinar.

"But Baba would be very disappointed if he knew we gave up without trying. He shouldn't be . . . his life must not be gone in vain," said Iora so resolutely that it surprised Chinar and Owlus.

With empty stomachs, a terrible grief, bruised limbs and a fistful of determination, they climbed down the shaky tree and cautiously began going downhill from the other side. They could no longer take the crumbling branch paths and aerial highways. It was also difficult to walk on the jungle floor as many branches fell down from above. The impact of the falling branches was minimised by the loops of lianas that tied the jungle in a tangle. It was not even noon and they had hardly progressed when winds began to whisper and then howl. Lianas began to snap due to the strong winds, allowing the massive branches a free fall. There was no place in sight where they could take shelter.

Iora saw a huge conifer with towering spikes that still stood more or less intact. She pointed it to Chinar and Owlus, and they ran towards it.

"Let's climb this!" shouted Iora, her long, black curls blowing all over her face with the wind.

Braving the blustery weather, they somehow managed to reach the top. It was the most difficult task Chinar had faced, more than being lost alone in the jungle. They clutched hard at the branches and witnessed the sad scene around them.

"There is no hope, this is the end," said Owlus with a heavy heart.

"Ma will keep waiting for me . . ." said Chinar, trying to hold back a sob.

Iora didn't say anything. She just sat there gazing into the murky sky and the dying forest.

A dark cloud of dust spread overhead, blocking the sun. The canopy swayed like a tossed wave in a torrential sea. A faint sound rose above the moaning wind.

"Did you hear that?" asked Iora.

"Hear what?"

Iora did not answer and became quiet. Again a soul stirring call rose above the din and this time it was heard by both Chinar and Owlus. They saw a dot floating towards them from afar and it grew larger and larger against the ominous grey backdrop.

"*Aquila anima*!" exclaimed Chinar.

It was indeed *Aquila anima*, the eagle bird spirit that roamed the forest with Thunderbird.

"What is it doing here?" asked Owlus, as it landed on a nearby tree.

Its wise red eyes, pristine black and silver feathers, curved yellow beak and high held head made it look majestic and out of the place in the disintegrating surroundings.

Aquila anima sat on an adjoining tree and extended one of its wings to the conifer so that it touched its canopy. It turned its head and looked at them intensely. Without hesitation, Iora got up, crawled on its wing and reached its back. Chinar and Owlus also climbed onto its back, one behind the other, balancing against the bellowing wind. The eagle spread its wings and gave a profound cry. Sparks came out of its silver feathers before it took off in flight. Flip-flop . . . it flapped its wings against the tough wind current.

"How did you know we were here?" asked Owlus, holding the eagle's back and hardly believing that they had been rescued.

"You know Baba was . . ." Iora started saying but fell silent.

Aquila anima kept flying in silence.

"Where are you taking us?" asked Chinar but didn't get a reply.

If this were in a different time and circumstance, they would have thoroughly enjoyed the flying experience.

But even this flight couldn't alleviate their sorrow of losing Baba. It even overshadowed the fact that it was the moonless night today and they still had not found the Spirit of the Jungle. The forest became more and more dreadful below them. Some patches had not just dried . . . they rather looked charred.

"Why . . ." asked Chinar.

"Dark forces are gaining power as the Animal Angel becomes weaker," said Owlus, terrified. "They've brought this to the forest . . . They must not succeed tonight!"

Till now *Homo-diabolus* was an obscure concept. But now they could see its powers and what it was capable of doing not just to them but to the whole jungle. They passed many rivers, which were reduced to thin quivering lines of water.

Before the evening fell, they reached the Scar-faced River and found it filled to the brim with water. The forest in this area was also the normal thick green mass. Troupes of monkeys, foraging birds, buzzing bees . . . everything was in order. Even the dark cloud of dust had cleared and they could see the sun on the horizon behind silky clouds. This sight lifted the heavy pall from their hearts.

"Everything is so normal here!" said Owlus; Chinar nodded with a faint smile.

"But why?" murmured Iora.

They had never felt that the jungle was so beautiful and so much a part of themselves.

The eagle reached a point near Twitterland on the side of the river where there was a large clearing, and began to glide over it. Trees were not cut down to make the clearing but they had been shrunken back to the sapling stage. This place brimmed with life. Sparks emitted from the clearing now and then. Iora realised it was from the sting of the Insect Angel. They understood why this place was not devoid of life – it was blessed with the presence of the Angels!

The Angels sat in a circle on the bank of the river. The Animal Angel looked frail and moved his snake tail with difficulty. The Bird Angel looked regal and stood tall with both her heads held high. The Aqua Angel had risen from the River and her stunning transparent figure glowed. Water flowed from both the sides of the Aqua Angel into the river. Perhaps that's why the Scar-faced River was full, thought Iora. The Insect Angel, who was in his giant form, sent a blazing light through his sting every now and then. But the Tree Angel could not be seen anywhere.

Webster, the six-eyed Insect Angel's guard, the Bird Angel's two sparrows and the moustachioed crab, Crabster, stood in alert around the circle of the Angels. Proboscis Porty, Fast Loris, baby elephant Emphuchi and a pack of black Leoparbees stood in guard behind the weak Animal Angel. Many figures of Twitters with their family birds were scattered on the fringes of the clearing, some on trees and others on ground. Iora looked hard to get a glimpse of her father but could not make out anything from that height.

"When are we going to get down?" she asked impatiently.

Aquila Anima didn't reply.

Thunderbird finally raised her head, looked at them and snapped her beak. *Aquila Anima* gave a profound cry and sparks came out of her silver feathers. It then took a downward plunge. Iora, Owlus and Chinar held on tightly to its feathers. Owlus thought he would fall down while landing, but the landing was very smooth. Without a jerk the eagle placed its claws firmly on the ground. They saw many Twitters and their family birds all around the periphery of the clearing. Some had climbed the trees to have a better view. They beheld the Angels in awe, not able to believe their good fortune. Iora, Chinar and Owlus bowed to the Angels, who stood near them in a circle. Webster, Emphuchi, Proboscis, Fast Loris and Crabster greeted them, all of them pleased at their sight. Emphuchi adjusted his tuft of hair, Proboscis munched incessantly and Webster's four eyes rolled over on the ground, observing all the things intently. They all were on alert.

"Where is the Tree Angel?" Iora asked the eagle, who was nearest to her.

But it simply gazed at the twilight sky.

Iora and Owlus turned to a figure running towards them from the periphery of the clearing. It was Heron!

Iora ran towards him and Heron picked her up from the ground in an embrace. Madame Flameback flew towards her and chirped happily, extending a wing to stroke her head. Fisherking and his wife also came running from a group of Twitters standing under the trees at the end of the clearing. Fowlus was also in the group but she stood rooted to the spot, afraid of coming too near to the Angels. Now it was Owlus's turn to be hugged and kissed by his parents. Chinar stood near *Aquila Anima*, looking longingly at both his friends meeting their families.

"Thank Angels you're fine!" Heron said, looking concernedly at Iora. "And thank Angels you're fine too," said Iora gingerly.

"Of course, now I'm fine since you're back!"

"The dark forces wanted your blood!"

"Grandpa Cockatoo told me you had got this idea after you were bitten by the Rogue Thorn Worm. I just returned three days ago. Father had sent me many Post Chimps but they could not reach me. You cannot imagine what it felt like when I heard you'd gone missing! You know your mother had also gone one such day and never came back . . ."

"Oh, Father . . ."

Madame Flameback looked at Heron with concern. But Heron regained control and smiled at Iora. Madame Flameback said in a lighter tone, "If Bungee Banyan had feet instead of roots, he would have run to meet you here!"

"How is Grandpa Cockatoo?"

"He's fine and awaiting you. He can't run like me, you know," said Heron, pointing towards a cluster of trees. "He had gone looking for you in the jungle but got no clue of your whereabouts. When I went to look for you I met Beetle on the way. He was coming to Twitterland to meet me."

"Beetle is okay!"

"Yes, he is quite fine and is with Grandpa. He said he was bedridden and suffering from partial memory loss, so he couldn't come earlier. He convinced me that you were in safe hands with Baba and would return on the moonless night. But where is Baba? I want to thank him!"

A dark cloud came over Iora's face and Heron realised something terrible had happened.

"Baba is . . . gone . . . trying to save my life . . ."

Before Heron could ask any more, Webster's voice boomed, "Moonless night has begun."

Everyone looked up at the greyish sky, which slowly turned a deathlike black.

"Why do you think the Tree Angel has not arrived as yet?" asked Thunderbird.

"I fail to understand . . ." trailed the Aqua Angel's voice.

"We cannot do anything without him," the Animal Angel said in a whisper.

The Insect Angel clicked his claws and multitude of firefly torches brilliantly lit up the clearing.

Owlus came to Iora with Chinar as Fisherking and his wife went back to join the other Twitters.

"I'm so sorry, Chinar; I didn't introduce you to my father. Father, Madame Flameback, this is my friend, Chinar."

Madame Flameback stared at him, shocked.

"Non-jungle dweller. We saw this boy the other day by the river," said Heron.

"Yes, the same one. There is so much to tell you Father!"

"And how are you doing, my boy!" said Heron, beaming at Owlus.

The ground beneath them shook slightly. A sapling emerged in the shallow waters of the river near the Aqua Angel and soon turned into a full-fledged tree with tiny star fruits budding from it.

"The Tree Angel is here!" said Owlus.

All the Angels looked relieved looking at the Tree Angel.

"About time, Tree," said the Insect Angel.

"There is destruction everywhere. I couldn't just ignore it on the way," replied the Angel rustling his leaves, his deep voice echoing in the surroundings.

The flaming plants with blonde hanging roots, which they'd seen around the Tree Angel, also emerged, lighting up the place further. The cluster of roots emerged with their pointed spikes ready for attack.

"We must begin only after it is completely dark," said the Aqua Angel, floating above the river.

"Must meet Grandpa and Beetle. I will be back before the Angels start, whatever they are going to start," said Iora and ran towards the trees. Madame Flameback flew back shaking her head at the non-jungle dweller.

Iora had to meet Cockatoo as she couldn't voice her thoughts even to her father. She resolved to ask her grandfather directly and settle her mind once and for all, even if it meant hurting him. She fervently wanted to be proven wrong just this once.

"I will also come and meet Beetle," said Owlus, running after her but then stopped midway. He couldn't face Beetle and break the news about Baba. So he returned to Chinar who stood awkwardly with Heron.

Beetle rushed to hug Iora when she reached the cluster of trees outside the clearing. This was quite away from the other groups of Twitters and they were blocked from the view.

"It is so relieving to see you fit and fine Beetle," she said as thoughts of Baba wracked her heart. She then hurried to meet her grandpa who stood in a dark corner under a tree.

"Grandpa?"

But there was no reply except a suppressed sob. Suspicious and guarded, Iora approached him with Beetle following behind. Cockatoo stood with his back at them, facing the tree trunk.

Iora cleared her throat, "Grandpa, please don't mind my asking this but there is something that I need you to tell me."

He still didn't reply.

"Don't be grumpy now, Cockatoo. Your granddaughter has achieved an enormous feat," said Beetle, oblivious of Iora's thoughts. He approached and touched him on the back.

Cockatoo slowly turned around and Iora saw an unexpected sight.

27
The Moonless Night

Cockatoo's face was smeared with tears. Iora had never seen him like that. "What's wrong, Grandpa?" she said, hurriedly coming to him, her mind devoid of all the previous suspicions.

"I am sorry, child. I've always been aloof with you . . . If something had happened . . . Thank Angels you've . . ." said Cockatoo, wiping his tears which wouldn't stop flowing.

His stern face looked much softer and older.

"Oh, Grandpa!" said Iora, hugging the old Twitter.

She felt very guilty and decided against asking him any baseless questions.

"I am so sorry, Grandpa. I really am!"

Her heart felt light after disposing off the terrible thoughts.

"Grandpa, I'll be right back. The Angels will start anytime."

"Carry on, child."

"Hello there!"

Kookaburra stood leaning on a tree a little away. He came forward and held her in an embrace.

"Hope you're fine, Kookaburra. I'll be back soon."

Iora tried to loosen his grip but Kookaburra didn't let her go.

"In a rush again, are you?" he said in an icy-cold voice.

"What's going on here, Kookaburra?" asked Beetle, approaching him.

"We'll hear your cynicism later, Kookaburra, let her go right now!" said Cockatoo.

"Shut up, you old hunched fool!"

Iora stared at Beetle and Cockatoo, and they both looked as astonished.

"Whom do you think you heard the other day when you were in the well, Iora?" Kookaburra continued in the same frosty voice.

He seemed powerful and not half-crippled with his joint pain.

"You were never so dense. Rather over-smart like your meddlesome mother!" said Kookaburra, his grip tightening as he gagged her mouth with one hand.

"Let her go. What has come over you?" said Cockatoo, shocked.

Beetle rushed towards both of them when something moved behind him. He turned hearing the sound.

A host of human figures slithering on the ground advanced towards them from three sides. They were totally covered in dry vines and fungi, which grew from their very bodies. Their faces were wrapped up in dry vines. Only their parched mouths and eyes were visible. Before they could cry for help, two human figures slithered towards Beetle and Cockatoo and grabbed them. Vines from their bodies grew instantly and covered Cockatoo's and Beetle's mouths. They were dragged behind the adjoining trees. Kookaburra followed with Iora in his grip.

***

"Let's finish it, quick!" commanded Kookaburra in a bitter voice. It was indeed this very voice she had heard outside the well that night.

"So, you ran wild, meeting the Angels! I should have finished this the night Chirkut came to me near the well. A great chance was lost to aid the great *Homo-diabolus* seventy years back. It was too late by the time I crushed those two Ghosts . . . damn those prying wasps! I'll make sure this time it doesn't go wrong!" mumbled Kookaburra, his eyes bulging out with malice, as he dragged her behind a cluster of trees.

The young Twitter, the unknown agent of *Homo-diabolus,* who had aided the anti-natural forces and killed the two Ghosts of Yellow Leaves was Kookaburra! Iora stared at him, horror-struck. She had not remotely suspected this half-witted old man. Yes . . . now the pieces fell into place – 'Cooka' was not Cockatoo but Kookaburra. She also remembered seeing Kookaburra dozing in his garden the night she was bitten by the Rogue Thorn Worm. The old Twitter's grip was so strong that she couldn't even fight back.

"Kill!" Kookaburra commanded the dark spirits, ". . . while I take her away."

The dark spirits gripping Beetle and Cockatoo spread the vines over their appalled faces. With one twist of their formless hands on their necks, it would be over. They were blocked from the view of the Angels and all other Twitters, who stood watching the Angels, spellbound. Iora knew she had to act now. There was not a fraction of a moment to lose. Her legs dangled near Kookaburra's knees. She knew his weak knee. Hoping it still was weak in spite of his dark powers, she kicked him hard on it.

He let out a painful grunt and his grip loosened. With all the might she had in her, Iora flung herself on the dark spirits and struck the one holding Beetle on its vine covered face. It jerked and left him. She then turned towards the one holding Cockatoo and hit it as well. It loosened its grip on Cockatoo but turned towards Iora and took her in its grip. Other spirits began to slither on the ground towards Beetle and Cockatoo who were both knocked out. Beetle stirred, coming to his senses, and struggled to get on his feet but was caught again by another creature and his mouth was covered with dry vines immediately. Kookaburra came towards them hurriedly, limping on one leg.

He held out his hands to take Iora, when a familiar voice rang in the air, "So we finally meet, Kookaburra."

Kookaburra turned in disbelief. "You're alive!"

Iora stopped struggling and looked in the direction of the warm, familiar voice. It was indeed Baba! Immense relief and joy flooded her, as no words would come out of her gagged mouth. Her most ardent wish had been granted – Baba was alive!

Baba stood with lightning in one hand, dazzling and sparkling as it moved, his other hand and legs placed firmly on the ground. He moved the lightning with an amazing speed at the dark spirits, which had started to creep towards him, and they all burnt down to ashes. Like a muffled thunder that follows each lightning, the gurgles of the spirits rose and fell after each strike.

"Release!" said Baba, pointing the lightning towards the creature suffocating Beetle. It let go of him. Beetle fell down in a heap. He got up and slowly moved towards Cockatoo who lay unconscious on the ground. The other dark spirits were stretched on the ground, with their heads raised and their vines clutching the earth, awaiting Kookaburra's next command.

"I will kill Iora if you don't stop, Baba!" Kookaburra's voice was a little shaky now.

Iora almost felt bad for him. She still couldn't believe

it was the same Kookaburra, the lonely Twitter whom everyone made fun of.

"Don't fool around. We both know you can't kill Iora; not now at least. Your revered *Homo-diabolus* will never forgive you if you do. Not only will you perish in pain but also have a terrible afterlife!"

Iora couldn't understand anything.

"Alright . . . now place her down."

But Kookaburra stood firm.

"Don't try me. The lightning is aimed straight at your head. You know how potent Thunderbird's weapon is!"

Kookaburra hesitantly released Iora and placed her on the ground. She stared at him incredulously. "What has got into you?"

But he didn't answer; rather he smiled most distastefully at her, scratching his unkempt beard.

"Come here at once, Iora!" said Baba.

She moved away from Kookaburra, turning to look at him again.

"Now you . . . you also come towards me quietly," Baba told Kookaburra.

He advanced reluctantly.

"Iora, are you there? What's taking you so long?" Heron called from behind the trees.

Kookaburra made a snarling sound and the rest of the dark spirits came slithering towards Baba, Beetle, Iora and Cockatoo, who lay knocked out on the ground. They rose from the ground and tried to catch Iora again.

Baba flashed his lightning thrice. Each time it took a novel shape, striking more than one spirit at once. Taking advantage of this confusion, Kookaburra disappeared.

"I will go and look for him!"

"No Beetle, not now. We are required by the Angels," said Baba.

Heron was dazed to say the least. What had he just witnessed! Before he could go forward to fight the vine-covered spirits they were all reduced to ashes by Baba. He rushed to Cockatoo and sat by him.

"What on earth is going on and who are you?" he asked.

"I am . . ." started Baba, but before he could complete, Iora broke in, "He is Baba, he's saved me once again from–"

Here she stopped, ran to Baba and hugged him tightly.

"Now, now . . . all is well, little one," said Baba, patting her.

Baba explained to Heron in brief about Kookaburra. Not giving him any time to absorb the shock, he dragged them to the clearing. Cockatoo regained consciousness and tried to stand up. Shaken, more mentally than physically, on discovering what his only friend had been up to for the last seventy years, he looked as pale as an old grave.

***

It seemed the Angels knew what had taken place.

Baba went and gave the lightning back to the Bird Angel who gulped it down her throat.

"Baba!" shrieked Owlus and Chinar. They ran towards him and hugged him, forgetting the Angels' awe-inspiring presence.

"You're okay! You're okay!" they shouted in chorus.

They shouted to Iora about Baba being alive but she stood glumly with Heron, Cockatoo and Beetle, looking taken aback herself. She had been immensely relieved that it was not her grandfather as she'd suspected, but she wasn't particularly happy about Kookaburra's revelation too – she'd known him since she was born.

"What's with them, Baba?" asked Owlus.

"Later, Owlus," Baba shushed him.

"Shall we?" boomed the Tree Angel's mystic voice.

Owlus and Chinar went and stood with Iora, Heron, Beetle and a frail-looking Cockatoo as Baba went near the Angels.

"Yes, it is time to start," said the Insect Angel, looking at the darkness and the starless sky.

"Iora, please approach," said the Aqua Angel in her sweet voice.

Iora looked puzzled but came to the Angel nevertheless.

"Oh no!" blurted Owlus, remembering the Spirit of the Jungle. "Get ready to die, Chinar!"

"Come to the centre, Iora," floated another recognisable voice.

It was *Homo-lamia*, whom Iora had met the other night on the branch and seen her sticky formless tongue. She peeped from behind the Bird Angel's talons.

"What are you doing here?"

Homo-lamia didn't answer but smiled sheepishly.

Something dawned on Iora. She recognised her familiar eyes and smile. These were the eyes of the horrible mermaid avoiding whom they'd dived in the cave of the Ghosts of Yellow Leaves just before the earthquake, of the three-horned chameleon who brought her up the tree just before the wild boars trampled the area, of the *Homo-lamia* in her true form when she consumed the lethal insects when they were about to bite her, of the strange woman who got *Homo-gigantis* to save them from Yaya's flesh eating garden . . . they all had the same eyes! It was *Homo-lamia* following her all along! She had changed form according to her monthly metamorphosis and appeared in different forms every time. But why was she following her all along and what was she doing with the Angels?

"Have you been able to find the Spirit of the Jungle?" the Aqua Angel asked.

Iora stood silent. Her mind was torn between shock of sudden recognition and speculating the consequences of not finding the Spirit of the Jungle. Owlus and Chinar stood edgily.

"Come to the centre, Iora."

Iora looked at Baba, who nodded reassuringly, and

went inside the circle of the Angels not knowing what to expect.

The Tree Angel extended two branches on either sides, stars dangling from them, towards the Water and the Bird Angel. The Aqua Angel extended both her translucent watery hands, the Bird Angel both her wings, the Insect Angel his front legs, and all of them held each other's hands. The Insect Angel and the Bird Angel were on either side of the Animal Angel. But instead of completing the circle by extending his front paws towards them, he walked slowly towards the centre.

Iora saw the Animal Angel closely as he came and stood near her. He had become much feebler and could hardly lift his gaunt face. Iora felt sorry to see such a majestic being in a miserable state.

Baba, Webster, Proboscis and other guards and spirits outside the circle retreated further away. They were stiff and alert. Webster's four eyes rolled towards the farthest corners of the clearing observing everything; Emphuchi no longer adjusted his hair; and Proboscis no longer munched. The groups of Twitters stood motionless in anticipation. Owlus and Chinar stood with Beetle, Heron and Cockatoo near the fringes of the clearing.

Iora had not replied. She thought hard, looking at the sky, staring at a star. Her eyes widened.

A star? But today there are no stars in the sky! thought Iora.

As she formed these words in her mind the star had

already grown to the size of a red glowing moon. The red round glow formed an outline of a fat-lipped drooping mouth in the sky. It seemed it was formed of fire and flesh and was of a deep scarlet colour.

"What is that?" she shouted.

Everyone looked up immediately. The mouth became more and more hideous. A fleshy forked tongue came out of it.

All the spirits of the Angels rushed towards the circle. Horror-filled shouts of Twitters rang in the air. It became stifling hot. Heron ran towards the Angels but couldn't reach Iora as she stood within the circle. Chinar, Owlus and Beetle huddled together, terrified. Cuckatoo looked anxiously at Heron and Iora. But the Angels kept holding each other's hands firmly and did nothing in defence.

"Hold the attack!" boomed the Insect Angel's voice addressing the spirits who had gathered around them.

"Why doesn't anyone do something?" Iora shouted.

The heat now burnt her skin. Red flames of ghastly shapes escaped the red mouth and sprang in all directions. The flames ran, leapt, soared and fumed in unearthly bewilderment. The sky was covered by this dance of death. The fiery forms grew in numbers as if the gates of nether world were left ajar. With skeleton arms stretched towards the Angel's circle, they descended from the sky towards them. The water of the river began evaporating due to the intense heat and steam rose in swirling clouds. A stifled cry came with a whooshing sound from the river and Iora turned to see a glimpse of Cuckatoo swaying in the air. A knuckle of steam had lifted him up the river. Hot water dripped from the grip, which tightened on Cuckatoo, and he was unable to shout due to the suffocation. Heron and others rushed to him. A hot wave from the river hit them with force.

Iora looked at the Aqua Angel imploringly, but she did not act. She wanted to rush out of the Angel's circle but the Aqua Angel said, "You cannot save him like this, Iora."

"Tell us immediately if you've been able to find the Spirit of the Jungle!" rustled the Tree Angel.

"But please stop these things first!"

"We can't break the Circle of Life now; we've to complete the missing link in the circle. It has to stand in place of the Animal Angel. There is no time to lose!" said the Bird Angel, looking at the infuriated sky.

Iora had not found the Spirit of the Jungle. What could she do now? Was there no other way to save Cockatoo? What would happen to the jungle?

"Oh yes!" she whispered, her eyes opening wide. A realisation struck her like lightning. She stood rooted on the spot for less than a second and then without answering the Insect Angel she dashed towards the empty spot in the Angels' Circle of Life. As she ran, the hideous figures with stretched arms let out unearthly moans. Their speed of descent increased and their hollow eyes and mouths became twisted with anger. The steam fist holding Cockatoo shook hard.

She reached the empty spot in the Circle and extended her hands on both sides holding the tip of the Bird Angel's wing and the Insect Angel's front leg. As soon as she did that, an amazing wave of energy surged inside her. She'd never felt so astonishingly light and full of life.

"Help us, dear Nature!" said all the Angels together as soon as she joined the circle. Clouds and thunder escaped the Bird Angel's beak and hung high above the Animal Angel. A fluorescent-coloured stream of water from the Aqua Angel rose and joined it. Twinkling stars from the Tree Angel and glittering sunrays from the silver sting of the Insect Angel also rose and coupled with the rest. The greenish-blue cluster looked spectacular. This cluster of stars, clouds, thunder, sunrays and water mingled to form a continuous green glow and started revolving overhead. Like the rush of floodwaters, this cluster attacked the approaching forms that had almost reached the Circle of Life. The mouth in the sky opened in a gruesome cry and the forked tongue got sucked in. The cluster then flew towards the ghastly hanging mouth. But before the mass could strike it, it extinguished and disappeared in the darkness. A call rolled away at a distance, as if someone was being strangled to death, and slowly faded into nothingness.

The mass gradually transformed into multi-coloured fluorescent fumes and soft streaks of light. This lighted up the jungle in various hues. Slowly, the bands of light and fumes descended towards the Animal Angel standing in the middle and penetrated him. The extreme heat died down and the surroundings became cool and fresh. The knuckle of steam evaporated, dropping Cuckatoo in the river. Heron jumped in and pulled him out.

The Animal Angel became stronger and stronger and by the time the whole cluster had disappeared into him he stood up in all his majesty, waved his nerve-racking snake tail and roared. The roar echoed in the jungle as his two long canines glistened in the dark. Again a rasping cry of some unnatural being rose and fell from far away. And then there was complete silence. The Animal Angel bowed to each of the four Angels and they also bowed in return. Stars appeared in the moonless sky. Fireflies came twinkling again and the torches got lit. The clearing was once again bathed in light.

28 The Dream

The Animal Angel turned to Iora and said, "You did it, little Twitter."

She didn't answer and looked in Cuckatoo's direction.

"He is alright," said the Aqua Angel.

Relieved to see him stand leaning on Heron, Iora bowed to the Aqua Angel and turned to the Animal Angel.

"We all did it together," she said, looking at Baba, Beetle, Chinar and Owlus.

The Twitters gathered again around the clearing. The Animal Angel smiled, exposing his glistening canines, and said, "You must be wondering why you are the Spirit of the Jungle."

Silence descended upon the all the gathered Twitters. Owlus, Chinar, Beetle, Heron and Cockatoo stood stunned.

"I was wondering why all the dark spirits and

Kookaburra tried to attack me and not Father as I'd thought. 'Heron's blood' . . . *I* was Heron's blood! I wondered why the dark forces were after me when I'd not even started on the Quest of Five. I could think of only one answer – I was the Spirit of the Jungle!" said Iora sceptically, not knowing if this enormous assumption was correct.

There were audible gasps from the groups of Twitters. Iora glowed with joy, not because she was the Spirit of the Jungle but because she'd found it at last and Owlus and Chinar wouldn't have to die along with her. She smiled at them but they seemed too shocked to realise that their lives and the jungle were just saved.

"Yes, you are right, little Iora," said the Aqua Angel.

"But why? What's there in me? I don't have any special powers . . ."

"You see the Bird Angel here, what is she?" the Animal Angel asked.

"Um . . . she is Thunderbird, who brings rain, makes vegetation grow, and sustains life."

"Yes, but above all she is Hope – hope with feathers. Hope that never gives up!"

Iora understood that but how did it make her the Spirit of the Jungle, she wondered.

"The Tree of Life here," continued the Animal Angel, "he's Wisdom, Wisdom with roots. There is nothing perfect in this world but faith. The Aqua Angel, she is Perfection – the timeless, formless, fathomless Faith.

The Insect Angel, well he is Balance – the Equilibrium of the forest. And I, Iora, am the Survival Instinct. The Survival Instinct with teeth – that fights all dangers and adversity!"

The Angel studied her for a moment and began again, "You must be wondering why I'm blowing my own trumpet. You may not be an Angel and not have our powers but you have an essence of each of us – solid faith in yourself, wisdom to put to use what you know and to learn what you don't, an uncanny survival instinct, an unfaltering hope and a measure of equilibrium to balance all the above. These are the qualities which make a living being whole. And you have them in perfect proportions."

Iora didn't know what to say.

She was still not convinced. "I am sure many jungle dwellers possess these qualities. The Angels would have to pick someone randomly like our 'Pick and Choose the Nut' game," she said.

The Angels smiled at her but didn't say anything.

"What is this *Homo-lamia* doing here?"

"*Homo-lamia* is your guardian," Baba came forward and said. "It was she in different forms trying to help you, right from the beginning when she saved you in the well when you were bitten by the Rogue Thorn Worm. She was in the aquatic animal state then, just after the moonless night. Every night during certain hours they resume their true form when they come out and hunt for sustenance. That was the time she saved you by consuming the deadly insects."

"Then why didn't she help us in the end?"

"*Homo-lamia* and *Homo-malus* lose their powers as the moon completes its cycle. As she could not help us any longer, she returned and informed the Bird Angel about your whereabouts so that *Aquila anima* could come to your rescue."

"The jungle is a stable entity, yet it is dynamic and changing every moment," said Thunderbird. "Being the Spirit of the Jungle is a beautiful thing, but it has its dangers as well. So you will be the Spirit of the Jungle for three more years. However, you will retain all your qualities always as those cannot be taken away," Thunderbird concluded.

Iora understood, bowed and then asked what had been troubling her for long, "But, my Angel, what had gone wrong last time when the two Ghosts of Yellow Leaves died?"

"Last time the two brave, simple-hearted People had got the whiff of some conspiracy going on like you did this time. But at that time the Spirit of the Jungle was a snake who was clueless about the dark forces and his own identity. That snake even assisted the People at one point to meet the Angels. But neither they nor the snake realised what he was, in spite of the numerous clues the forest and his guardian, *Homo-malus*, gave to him and the boys. It was sad, but Nature can only guide.

One's destiny is in one's own hands. Kookaburra killed them both but it was too late, as they had succeeded in informing all the Angels to gather. Our other spirits like Webster and Crabster could not protect the two boys because we had to use all these Spirits together in place of the Spirit of the Jungle, which was not present, to form the Circle of Life. However, the dark forces also could not find the Spirit of the Jungle and use it to stop or hinder us."

"How can we help clear the name of the Ghosts of Yellow Leaves, Angel?"

"Nature has taken care of that. As the forest dried and disintegrated in the last two days, many jungle tribes like the Pebbles, Head Hunters, Amazons, and *Homo-avis* were given shelter by Vipero and the People in their underground caves. Especially creatures like Bara, your *Homo-avis* friend, and his tribe, who stay at the top layers of the forest, were the most venerable. The trust of the jungle denizens has been restored in the People."

"But we must warn the jungle here," rustled the Tree Angel, "that the near victory of two times in a short span of hundred years has left *Homo-diabolus* defeated, but not as weak as before. And he has his trusted agents like Kookaburra at large."

"He said he had done something to my mother . . . what had he done?"

Heron looked at them wide-eyed.

"That, little one, only Nature will reveal with time."

Iora still couldn't accept that Kookaburra could be so evil.

The Aqua Angel said benignly before she'd voiced her feelings, "Kookaburra had always had a sly and evil streak in him. Everyone has right to make their own choices in life. Kookaburra made his choice all those years back and you made yours when you went searching for the 'Five'. It is your choice today also – you can either feel bad about his treachery or be happy that you and your father are safe, and your grandfather is not what you thought him to be."

Iora looked at her in surprise.

Fisherking advanced towards the Angels; he looked exultant beyond words.

He bowed to them and said, "Words fail me at such a heavenly sight . . . I had never imagined that I would be able to behold even *one* Angel in my lifetime! We are indeed grateful to Iora. My soul flutters with joy as I thank you on behalf of all the Twitters for blessing us with your presence!"

He bowed so low that his nose almost touched his knees. All the other Twitters approached and stood in reverence.

"Thank you Fisherking and Twitters for having us and may the forest bless you all!" said the Bird Angel.

"One last thing before you go, my Angel," said Iora, sensing that the gathering was about to end. She turned to the Tree Angel and asked, "Why 'three friends'? Why Chinar?"

"Well . . . your fellowship with a non-jungle dweller is a reminder that the jungles, mountains, deserts and all civilisations of the world are interdependent. The destruction of one will lead to the destruction of the other."

The whole gathering looked towards Chinar and he felt blood rushing to his cheeks.

"But Angel, what if he betrays your trust and reveals our whereabouts to the other non-jungle dwellers?" asked Toucan boldly from a distance.

"What do you have to say about this, Chinar?" rustled the Tree Angel.

"Angel, if you do not want me to tell anything to my folks, I swear won't. I will never say a word about it to anyone and will not place those who've helped me in danger!"

"I will be responsible to the jungle if I've placed my trust wrongly in this boy. I can sense that the future may hold this fellowship dear," the Tree Angel's words floated with the breeze.

Many Twitters still eyed Chinar with suspicion. He averted his gaze and looked at the Aqua Angel instead. Her sight calmed him.

"I know you want to go back to your parents, Chinar," said the Aqua Angel, "but I regret to inform that your father has left after searching for you for days."

Chinar stood shell-shocked. Iora and Owlus looked at each other. Chinar had absolute faith that he would find his people once the task was done. Tears welled in his eyes but he tried to control himself.

"Do not be saddened. Believe in Nature."

The Aqua Angel turned to other Angels. "So long, friends. Long Live the Jungle!"

Twitters saw the Aqua Angel become one with the waters of the Scar-faced River. Crabster also got into the river after her.

The rest of the Angels bid farewell to each other and hailed the forest before departing. The Bird Angel spread her wings and took off in flight. The two sparrows and *Aquila anima* followed her close behind. The Animal Angel leapt on one of the trees and disappeared in the dark beyond. Proboscis, Emphuchi and Fast Loris took after him. The black Leoparbees took off in a noiseless flight and were gone in a jiffy. The Tree Angel and his plants with glowing hanging roots reduced themselves to saplings and disappeared in the ground with the cluster of roots. The Insect Angel stretched his metallic black wings and flew away with Webster trotting in the same direction. All of Webster's eyes were placed neatly in their respective sockets now.

Baba turned towards Iora who had joined Heron, Cockatoo, Beetle, Owlus and Chinar. Iora and Owlus felt terribly bad for Chinar but didn't know how to show their concern.

"Come here, little one," said Baba. Chinar came to him, his lips quivering. "We are here for you. Never be hopeless or dreamless in life. And I hope your people also believe in dreams."

"We thought you were gone . . ." said Owlus after a moment's silence.

"I was saved because the Aqua Angel protected me. She knew I couldn't swim properly and when we had met her, she blessed me against drowning. You remember she drenched me with her divine water when she splashed back in the water body? That is why I didn't drown and could fight that ancient water creature. I lay unconscious under that deep waterhole for many hours."

"Oh . . ."

"I must go now."

"You can't go!" said Iora.

"You must stay with us!" Owlus insisted.

"That is an impossible proposition, little ones." Baba turned to Chinar again and said, "Be as brave as you have been. Remember . . . everything passes. Here . . . take this."

He took out a neatly folded bark packet from under his long hair and placed it in Chinar's hand. He carefully opened it to see a little dirty white cocoon. Fearing that he would start crying if he spoke, Chinar just looked at Baba questioningly. Baba tapped on the cocoon three times.

The cocoon stirred. A crack surfaced on it and a shiny

black caterpillar came out of it on Chinar's palm. It had a green flame flickering on its head. A tiny illuminating golden seed rolled on its back as it moved. The three children looked at it with wonder. With his long finger Baba tapped on the cocoon again and the caterpillar went inside it. The cocoon closed once it was within.

"Tap on the cocoon when you need to get to me. Once the caterpillar comes out recite these lines – 'The moon is sad and the sun is pale. Have to catch the falling star's tail.' It will guide you to me."

"The moon is sad and the sun is pale. Have to catch the falling star's tail," Chinar recited after Baba in a barely audible whisper.

"That's right. I must get going now."

Baba patted the three children on their heads and turned to go. "May Nature be with you."

"When will we see you again?" Iora's voice was heavy.

"When Nature will want us to meet."

The trees which had un-grown to saplings to make the clearing re-grew at a fast pace. Baba disappeared behind the re-growing trees.

Iora and Owlus turned to Chinar who looked after Baba silently. The trees had re-grown and stood lofty and majestic as ever. Fisherking requested his wife as well as the other Twitters and the family birds to return to Twitterland and prepare for festivities. The Twitters could speak to Iora and Owlus there, he told them. Madame Flameback flew overhead and cast a confused look at Chinar. She was torn between pity for the lost child and her age old hatred for the non-jungle dwellers. With one last glance she flew back to Twitterland. Soon all the Twitters and family birds had retreated from the surrounding jungle. Fisherking came towards Heron and Cockatoo who stood talking to the three children and Beetle.

Iora remembered something. "Where is Hoatzin, Father?" she asked.

"Well, she is the one who informed us to gather here tonight. But she herself went again to the jungle today morning it seems."

"Oh no . . . Where has she gone? There is so much to ask her . . . You know she rescued us from Amazonland!"

Iora noticed a shadow pass over Heron's face at the mention of Amazonland. But he quickly gave her a broad smile and tapped her head.

Fisherking stood near Heron beaming. "Iora, Owlus and Chin . . . Chinar, I would like to thank all of you . . . What is that?" Fisherking looked around in alert.

A sound rose from some distance in the river. Beetle swiftly climbed an adjoining tree and came back within moments.

"It is a transport of non-jungle dwellers!"

"Chinnnnaaaaar . . ." echoed someone's tired voice.

Within moments all except Chinar had hidden in the in the shadows.

The cry came again, now in a different voice.

Chinar didn't know what to do. He became so excited and jittery that by the expression of his face he looked horror-struck.

"Hamza is calling! My father is calling! They are here!"

He darted towards the bank of the river, falling down and getting up a couple of times. The boat came into view down the river and he saw searchlights beaming.

"Papa! Hamza!" he hollered with all the strength.

The amazement of the boat crew on finding him was so great that for a minute or two they just pointed the light in his direction and stared blankly. A middle-aged man with salt and pepper hair and a thin moustache, a young man with binoculars and a couple of dark-skinned natives stood on the deck of a blue and white cruiser along with their captain.

The boat was immediately hauled to the shore. Hamza and Dr Reddy came running towards the little boy clad in a loincloth of bark. The Captain followed them brushing his bushy white moustache in excitement and wonder.

"Chinar! Chinar!" Dr Reddy repeated frantically as he held him.

Hamza gave him a bear hug and the Captain shook his hand warmly.

"This is a miracle! I thought I'll never see you again," faltered Dr Reddy.

"How did you find me?" Chinar managed to ask in a chocked voice.

Dr Reddy was too overwhelmed to reply so the Captain

volunteered, "We thought Hamza had gone raving mad when he said we will find Chinar just where we'd lost him. We'd never seen the shy Hamza firm to the extent of being fanatical. We'd searched you for days until we lost all hope of finding you. We were already two and a half days in the sea. On his insistence we headed back. I am so happy we did!"

"Why did you want to come back, Hamza?" asked a surprised Chinar.

"I had a dream, Chi-Chinar. There was a large ape . . . an orangutan in it. He told me where to fe-find you and when. Something within me said I had to do as the ape said. I believe there are unknown marvels of nature on whose face our common sense would stand laughing. I knew it was be-beyond logic . . . but I made sure we come back!" Hamza beamed at him.

It was Baba who came in Hamza's dream! How did he do that? Chinar wondered, silently clutching the bark packet that Baba had given him.

A feeling of extreme gratefulness flooded Chinar. He so much wanted to thank Baba and his friends. He looked around the river but only the dark green foliage looked back at him. The Twitters were masters in concealing themselves.

Though he still stammered, Chinar had not seen Hamza so confident ever. Chinar knew his friends would be listening to every word of the conversation. Iora understood a little Hindi and Chinar spoke loudly so that she could hear and understand. And sure enough she did, most of the talk. She translated it to Beetle and Owlus who hid near her looking at the non-jungle dwellers in wonder.

"Now you should tell us. How did you manage to survive these long days in the jungle? And what are you wearing?" asked the Captain with deep curiosity.

Chinar thought for a second and said, "I remembered what Papa used to tell me and the books he read to me. I could understand the ways of the rainforest. And the forest was very hospitable. Will tell later, but before that you must promise to bring me along every year on your expeditions here. Even if you're coming in six months' time you must coincide your plans with my half yearly school holidays..." he beseeched his father.

"We'll see about that. After being stuck in this awful place and escaping death, I am surprised you want to come here again," said Dr Reddy, regaining his old authoritative voice.

"The rainforest is very kind, in contrast to what we think of it."

"Young man, you are quite imaginative, but anyway your survival here will make quite a story. Do not be surprised if TV programs on survival approach you. Well, okay, I'll try to bring you along whenever I come this way. I am sure you would have gained some perspective about the rainforest flora in your stay. It may be valuable for my study," said Dr Reddy matter-of-factly.

"Shall we get moving now?" asked the Captain.

"Yes, just a minute, let me thank the forest," Chinar turned around and shouted, "Thank you so very much friends, goodbye! We will meet soon!" in Jungly.

He felt guilty that he had acted so rash and didn't even say a proper goodbye before rushing towards the boat.

His people didn't understand the gibberish but no one ventured to ask him anything. He waved at the jungle and climbed the boat.

***

As the unnatural sounds of the boat receded, six forms emerged from darkness and turned homewards.

"Thank Nature the boy has returned home!" trailed Cuckatoo's voice.

"Indeed," added Fisherking. Heron also nodded and smiled.

"I feel happy for Chinar but sad also. It would have been good if we'd spent some more time together . . ." said Iora.

"Yeah I know. Will miss the old drag," said Owlus. "Anyway, I knew Baba had something in mind regarding Chinar, you know."

"Like ghost's grandmother you did! And look who's talking about missing Chinar! Let me refresh your memory when you said you'd listen to the Boobook sisters' gossip rather than 'old spring mouth's' non-stop-nonsense! You said you couldn't wait till his old wicked father took him back across the seas . . ."

"Oh yeah, Miss fat Spirit of the Jungle, I think the Angels mistook you for the swell-headed three-horned . . ."

"Now will you two cut it out!" boomed Beetle's voice as they disappeared in the thick of the dozing rainforest.